Sahul

From the first footprint
on an Australian beach,
to the discovery of a continent.

GRAHAM SCHAFER

A catalogue record for this book is available from the National Library of Australia

Publisher:
ASPG (Australian Self Publishing Group)
P.O. Box 159, Calwell, ACT Australia 2905
Email: publishaspg@gmail.com
http://www.inspiringpublishers.com
National Library of Australia Cataloguing-in-Publication entry

Author: Graham Schafer

Title: **SAHUL**
    From the first footprint on an Australian beach, to the discovery of a continent.

Cover Designer: Virgil Petrini

ISBN: 978-1-923449-56-5 (print)
ISBN: 978-1-923449-57-2 (ePub2)

Acknowledgement

This is to acknowledge my friend and editor, Dr. Michael Kavanagh. Without his editing skills, support and encouragement this book would never have been written.

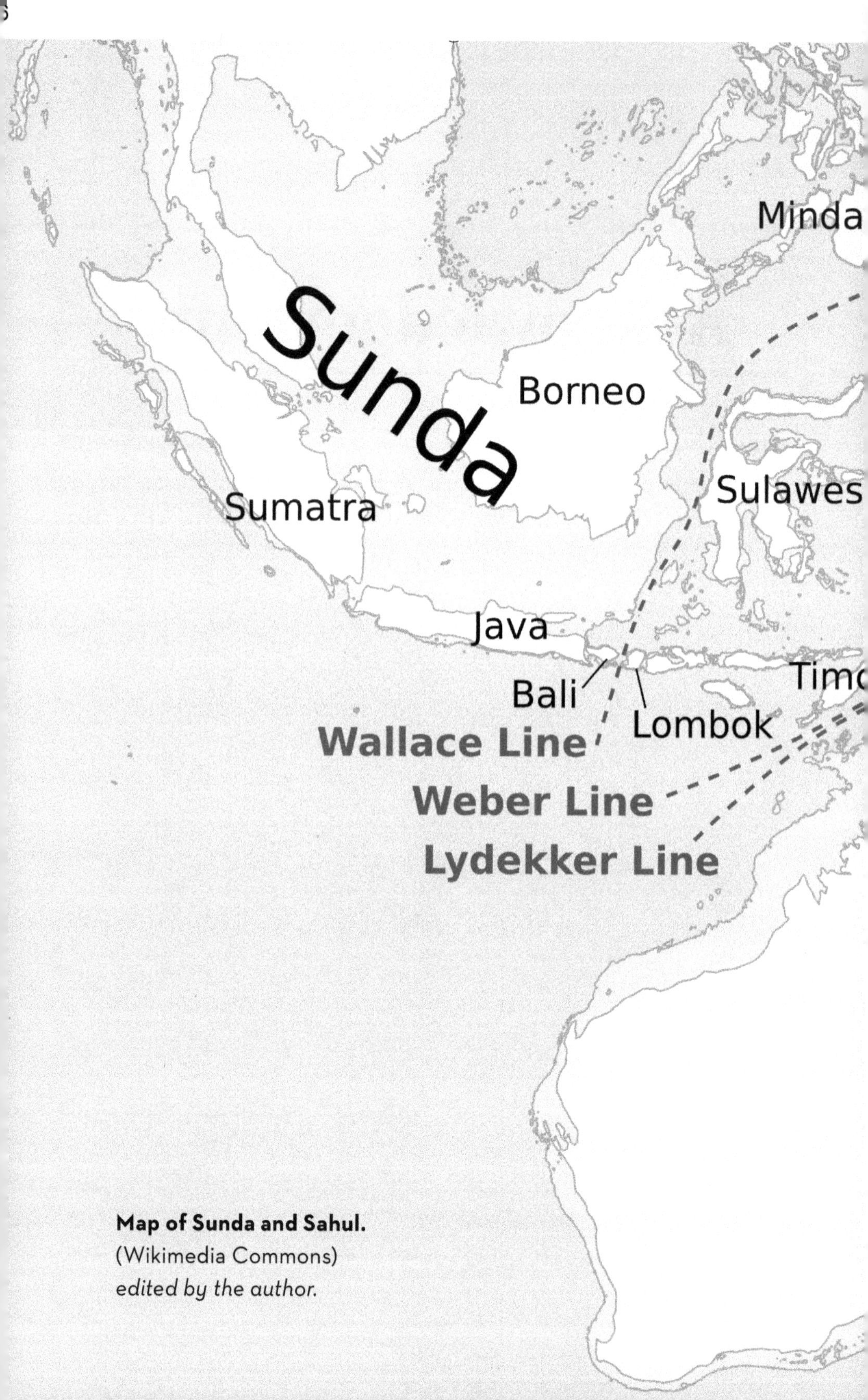

Map of Sunda and Sahul.
(Wikimedia Commons)
edited by the author.

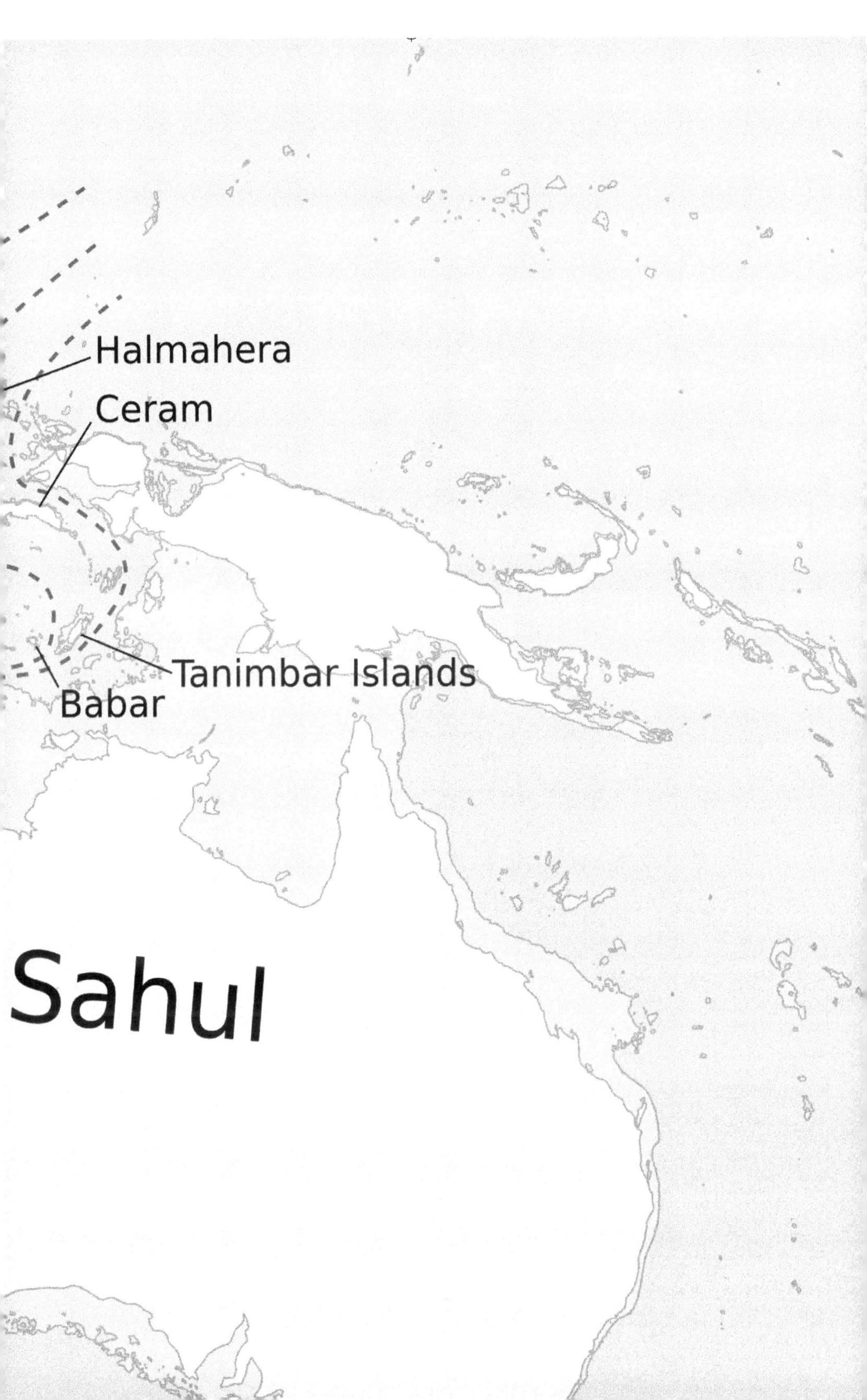

Halmahera
Ceram
Babar
Tanimbar Islands
Sahul

About the Author

Graham was born in London during the second world war. He left school at fifteen and completed an engineering apprenticeship with the Fairey Aviation Company in 1966. Graham emigrated to Australia with his wife Sonia in 1969, settling in Melbourne. He has two adult daughters. Graham started to write short stories in 2019. This is his first published work.

Preface

This adult story is fictitious. It is set during a time of very low sea levels, when Papua New Guinea, Australia, and Tasmania were joined together into a supercontinent called Sahul.

The story is about the first intercontinental sea voyage in human history, and the people who made it.

The earthquake in the story is the super-volcanic eruption of Mt Toba in Sumatra, which took place approximately 74-70 ka. (Thousand years ago)

The island in the story is very much like Timor.

Information regarding the building of bamboo rafts with stone tools was obtained from the internet and YouTube videos.

Very valuable information regarding the progress out of Africa of Homo sapiens and the life of Stone Age hunter-gatherers was gained from 'The Original Australians 2019' by Josephine Flood.

"It is probable that, throughout prehistory, a trickle of people made landfall on Australia's coast, but genome studies indicate that present-day Aboriginal Australians are descended from the first people to appear in the Australian archaeological record and that the founding population was very small, possibly numbering only between 50 and 70 people."

"Sometime between 70- 65 ka the first human footprint appeared on an Australian beach."

This is that story.

Sahul
Part 1

Four men of the Dwayne were making white ochre in the clearing by the river bank, close to their camp by the river estuary. They had flat rock pallets and flint axe head grinders. Tuan at seventeen was the eldest of the group. Earlier that day, he had swum in the river and then dived down to collect the soft white clay that was embedded in the river bank. He had made several trips and soon had sufficient clay which he placed on large flat leaves in the shade of the palm trees. Shortly, the others arrived. Lay, Parpi, both fifteen, and Brun, who had just been initiated into manhood, started to work. They mixed the clay with a little water and ground the large lumps of clay with their axe head grinders against their flat rock pallets into a fine white paste. Tuan knew they would need the ochre soon for the ceremonies of the tribe. These young men worked hard all morning with their lithe naked brown bodies dripping with sweat. It was about midday and the sun was hot, so they stopped to rest under the shade of the palm trees.

Tuan lived with his father Tanute, his mother Wayba, his fourteen-year-old sister Tara, and brother Vashna, who was ten, and their extended family of the Tanute clan. Tuan did not get on well with his father thinking him lazy and too fond of the krrack spirit the men made from grains, fruit, and fermented coconut sugar. Tuan hated the thick brownish liquid and he would never drink it. Tuan loved his mother well enough, but it was his sister Tara that he loved more than anything else. He felt it his duty to protect her, and the men of the tribe had always understood that she was not available. Lay and Parpi were Tuan's cousins. They loved making the bamboo rafts used by the tribe for fishing amongst the coral reefs. Brun was a friend, and member of the Odaa-nas, the other clan of the Dwayne. Tuan had little to do with Vashna, who contented himself with playing in the rainforest and helping his father. Tuan sometimes felt that he did not quite fit in with the other men of the tribe, and it was sometimes remarked that he resembled the men of the Tarawa, the mountain tribe of the north, being much taller than the stocky men of the Dwayne.

One day, the men felt a faint earth tremor, nothing unusual about that, given there had been tremors for weeks, however, the tribe's medicine woman Fryer had recently been prophesying doom. Colourful birds squeaked, and with a massive flapping of wings flew from their shelter in the jungle canopy. The earth shook terrifyingly, and a shock wave tore through the trees, high branches snapping and crashing to the ground. The young men jumped up and looked at each other in terror.

"Earthquake! Earthquake!" screamed the boys.

They fled down the narrow jungle pathway, down through the forest, jumping over branches, with Tuan leading the way, and Parpi, Lay and Brun, not far behind. Soon the pathway swung to the right, opening up to the vista of a broad white sandy beach, stretching to the left, around a bay of brilliant turquoise sea and disappearing towards a high headland. They could see the women in the distance. The two captive women Oc and Tat were on the beach. Tara with her friend Zika in water up to their waists. Tara was holding her baby boy Payu, but something was wrong. Oc and Tat swung around and raced up the beach towards the tree line with Zika. As they watched, the water level dropped rapidly exposing the inner coral reef.

"Tsunami!"

Tuan frantically screamed at his sister, warning her to get to higher ground. But she did not hear him. She stood frozen, holding her baby, and looking out to sea at the wall of water heading straight towards her at frightening speed.

The men were swept up by the huge wave and deposited into the forest. They had been through a terrifying ordeal of white water, rocks, stones, vines and an amazing assortment of fish. It had happened so fast. Tuan was stunned and found himself wedged between the lower branches of a tree. Parpi was alive and close but tangled up in vines. Tuan could hear him moaning. Tuan turned, and sliding down, crawled through the mass of grasping undergrowth to Parpi,

"Anything broken?" he asked.

"The women! Find the women!" groaned Parpi.

Tuan called out,

"Lay! Brun!"

But there was no reply, and Lay and Brun were nowhere to be seen. The forest edge had been devastated, with huge trees uprooted with mud and debris scattered everywhere. Tuan's mind raced with questions. How do we get out of this mess? Is this a visitation from evil spirits? Have my sister Tara and Lay, Brun and the captive women survived?"

Tara had been engulfed by the wave, but she was an excellent swimmer, and tightly clutching her baby under one arm and holding her breath she made a desperate lunge, and struck out freestyle with the other arm. Tara thought her lungs would burst. Tara surfaced, gulped a breath, and went under again. Before Tara knew it she was deposited on open ground above the beach. Her friend Zika and the captives Oc and Tat were there as well. It was a miracle they had all

survived, but the child was unconscious. Zika was semi-conscious and coughing up water. Oc crawled towards Tara and the baby through the tangled foliage and mud. Oc was scratched and bruised but reached out to Payu, who was still under his mother's arm. She laid the small child out and started expelling water from his lungs. Payu began to cough and splutter as water drained from his tiny body.

Nearby, Tat discovered she had a deep gash over her forehead, but even worse she had lost a precious necklace torn off in the tsunami. She scratched around in the undergrowth in a vain attempt to find it. Tara's body was also badly scratched and bruised, and she had a deep gash on her right hand. Tara and Oc lay down together exhausted, and cried.

"Oc, you have saved the life of Payu," gasped Tara.

But Oc, the Wollon did not completely understand the Dwayne language, so she kissed her tenderly and held her hand.

A month before the earthquake, the tribe had experienced the ritual of the White Snake, the tribe's totem. The headmen of the tribe, including Tanute, sat in a circle around a fire beating drums of hollow tree trunks. Other men played reed pipes. They watched about twenty selected women in a long line singing a monotonous chant and dancing to the hypnotic music. The women naked and covered in white ochre, wove the intricate movements of the snake ceremony, weaving through the assembled tribe. Some initiated men and girls, fourteen years old for boys, and eleven years old for girls, had taken part in the ritual for the first time. The ritual was undertaken to strengthen the tribe for war.

The neighbouring tribe, along the west coast and beyond the high headland had been encroaching on their territory. Members of this tribe had desecrated the paintings of animals, hunters, and totem spirits on the roof of the red rock shelter. A site that was sacred to the tribe. It was time for payback. That tribe was the Wollon, whose men covered their bodies in black pigment and pierced their ears, noses, and mouths, to enable them to hang the bones and teeth of deceased relatives upon their bodies. They were cannibals, who, in times gone by, raided the Dewayne, and stole their women.

The tribe of the Dewayne had lived on the island for centuries. Their semi-permanent camp was on a ridge, on the western bank of a tranquil river, which backed up onto a lagoon before gently trickling down to a wide estuary. It was a long narrow island with a high mountain range in the north. It had a tropical climate and a monsoon season from November to April.

The people of the Dewayne were semi-nomadic hunter-gatherers. A short stocky race with set laws and customs, not prone to disease or misfortune and well-adapted to their rainforest home. They were naked, but the women would often wear an amulet around their necks containing totems, and sometimes a wicker basket or strap for holding a baby, worn diagonally over the right shoulder. The tribe had no marriage custom. A man could choose any initiated woman and she would be expected to submit, not just to him but to any man that was attracted to her. They were handsome people, with straight black hair, and healthy brown bodies. The women had full round faces with large brown eyes, small wide noses and full lips. The men were usually taller than the women, with quite stocky bodies, long legs, and slightly elongated faces. They had deep-set eyes, wide mouths and straight noses with wide nostrils. It was fashionable for young men to cut their hair at about shoulder length and tie it in a bun at the back. Tuan, like many Dwayne men who had come of age, used his hair bun to store small religious artefacts like crocodile teeth or small pieces of white snakeskin.

Tuan had been a child prodigy, quickly learning from the men to hunt, lay traps, make stone tools, and how to avoid the many dangerous animals in the forest, such as crocodiles and poisonous snakes. The women taught him how to cook, choosing what was edible food and the herbs to use as medicine. He learnt how to render palm tree fibre into soft material for making matting, sails, and baskets. He remembered it all.

Tuan had a special teacher. The shaman, Cleft-ta, taught him the laws, spirits and totems of the tribe. He was taught the responsibilities of men and women, especially the customs that dictated that men would hunt and fish, while women would dig for tubas, gather fruit, and shellfish and look after children. Cleft-ta taught him about the phases of the moon, about eclipses, the night sky, and how to navigate by the stars. Cleft-ta had taken it upon himself to educate the very clever son of his friend Ta-nute, but at some point Cleft-ta would expect a favour.

Tuan had a sweet tooth and discovered how to calm bees with smoke to harvest wild honey. The young girls loved him and wove honey baskets for him. Tuan remembered going on trading expeditions with his uncle Uepti towards the mountains, when he was seven, and getting to know the people of the mountains, the tribe of the Tarawa. Tuan soon picked up some of their language.

I n time, he would become fluent in the Tarawa tongue and learn from them the finer and more intricate art of flint napping to make especially fine stone tools. When he was ten, he spent much time perfecting a small blowpipe, to make it more accurate. He devised a way to cut concentric bevels on the darts to make them spin when blown and accurately hit the intended target.

It was the rainy season, so it was not usual for dark and threatening clouds to appear at lightning speed, with thunderclaps and sheets of heavy rain. It was raining the night of the council of war. Freya, the old medicine woman was still predicting doom and casting spells. The meeting included Tuan, his father Tar-nute, the shaman, Cleft-ta, and Wurk, a brave hunter. Some other men of the tribe, Tobo, Tarasti, and Boni also attended. It was all agreed that the Wollon should be taught a lesson, for although they were a fearsome tribe, the men of the Dewayne regarded them as stupid and ignorant savages, who could not swim or make rafts. There had been a rowdy exchange of views about tactics and objectives. Some favoured a frontal attack directly through the forest, others favoured an attack from the sea using the tribe's bamboo rafts.

"We should do both," said Tuan. "I will go with Lay, Parpi and about five other men as if we intend to raid the Wollon camp in the forest near the red rocks."

He suggested that this diversion should draw out the Wollon tribesmen from their other camps.

"We will not go so far as to fall into a trap or ambush," he continued.

"Our very best young warriors, led by Wurk, can then silently paddle down the coast beyond the high headland on the rafts and attack the Wollon camp. That should teach them a lesson not to mess with us."

They were prepared to kill any men they found, and destroy and burn their totems; taking anything useful like spears or women. They would wait for the new moon and a dark night.

After waiting several days, the time was at last right for Tuan to lead his band of warriors through the rainforest, towards the territory of the Wollon. A rainforest like no other, containing enormous cabbage trees, prehistoric plants with gigantic leaves and vines intertwined with very tall trees and ferns. This special forest boasts an amazing array of insects, including huge colourful butterflies, snakes, giant Komodo dragons, hummingbirds, and even dangerous tapirs. They were well prepared with spears, and Tuan had bought his blowpipe darts and poison. They had painted themselves with red and white ochre for disguise, and Cleft-tar made a sacrifice to the White Snake God of grains and spices. Sandalwood burned on a ritual fire.

The band was led by the tribe's best tracker, the old man Bandawaa. It would take them about two days to reach the Wollon territory because the old tracks were overgrown and new ones had to be cut, no easy task with only stone hatchets and knives. They needed to make good time to coordinate their attack with the men on the rafts. Despite periods of torrential rain they had made good progress.

It was dawn on the second day, and Lay, had woken up with sunlight streaming through the leaves of their temporary shelter, and to a wonderful chorus of bird songs. He looked out to see sunlight sparkling on the raindrops causing a profusion of tiny rainbows. Lay, and Parpi, scrambled out to find breakfast. They came back with tortoise, black tree mushrooms, and fruit.

Tuan made a fire with dry kindling, and they were soon enjoying roast tortoises, and mushrooms, washed down with delicious papaya juice. Other members of the group had found lizards, termites, and a brush turkey to roast, as well as berries and fruit, like Rambutan and Pomelo. The bounty of the forest.

"Time to move on," called Tuan and the little band of warriors moved on with Ban-da-waa in the lead, cutting his way through the overgrown track. Further along the track, they reached a clearing, where trees had been felled by lightning. They moved on down the track through low-lying vegetation. Suddenly, all became still and quiet. Bandawaa raised his right hand to stop. Terror charged through the old man's body as he looked into the eyes of a huge Quinkana, a gargantuan terrestrial crocodile crouching low and almost completely camouflaged in the undergrowth. In a flurry of crashing foliage and branches, the Quinkana sprang, and opening its massive jaws took the old man in its mouth, spraying blood and foam over the terrified group. There had not been time to throw a spear and in a blink of an eye, Bandawaa and the beast were gone.

After they had recovered their composure they moved on, but after a short time one of the men, Dattawaa, the new guide, became ill. Within an hour he died screaming in agony. Whatever he ate must have been poisonous. They quickly disposed of the mushrooms and berries he had been eating. The omens were telling them to go back, what should they do? Then a small white snake was found half-eaten by a lizard. There was no doubt in Tuan's mind that they must return, and so they did.

Getting closer to the Dewayne encampment by the river, Tuan's companions heard the sound of drums, pipes, and rhythm sticks. There was a huge celebration, men on the bamboo rafts, led by Wurk, had

won a tremendous victory for the tribe. They had taken the Wollon completely by surprise. They had killed five Wollon warriors and their witch doctor, and destroyed many totems. They arrived back at camp a with booty of dried meat, fish, a basket of red ochre, spears and beads. They had also taken two women captive. The celebrations would go on for days. And so Tuan was back with his mother and father. Tar-nut and Wayba welcomed him home and comforted him for he was still in shock.

The Dewayne campsite had been spared much of the devastation of the tsunami situated as it was on higher ground some way back from the estuary. Tuan, Lay and Parpi had been rescued, but there had been casualties. Some women who had been foraging for edible roots and tubers near the estuary were missing, along with Vashna, but later that day Brun had been found some way off, unconscious. Tara, baby Payu, Zika, Oc and Tat had been rescued from the rubble and devastation.

Back at the camp, Freya and Miro her assistant, were dressing wounds and applying splints to those with broken bones. It was a fearful time for everyone. When Tara and baby Payu were sufficiently recovered Tara went to find her mother and father. Wayba had been in the forest collecting fruit with other women and they all made it back to the camp. They found their home in a state of confusion. Tara soon found her mother and gave her Payu to look after while she went to look for her father. She could not find him and walked for quite a distance beside the river towards the estuary. Soon she started to feel sick and confused and stopped to sleep near the river.

✦

Tara woke up with a terrible thirst and went to the river to drink. Then something caught her eye. In the distance, on a mudflat, she could see someone motionless, surrounded by vultures. She went to investigate, only to find the half-eaten body of her brother, Vashna. She screamed in horror.

Meanwhile, Oc took some time to get over the shock. She was only scratched and bruised, but she was badly shaken and feeling nauseous. Clearing away some rubble, she lay in the shade of some small trees near Freya's lean-to. The flies were a nuisance and she brushed them away with a fern leaf. She contemplated how her life had changed since she had been captured in the raid on the Wollon.

She was a handsome young girl, quite short with tight curly brown hair, large brown eyes, full lips, and a well-proportioned body. She was sixteen years old and had lived with an aunt, who sold her body to the Wollon men. And was raped by many more. Her ears and nose had been pierced at a young age to hang bone beads. Oc proudly wore a necklace of snail shells that she had made and painted herself with blue, red, and white ochre. She had never had a child, but loved children and loved looking after children from the tribe. She had put up no resistance to being captured. For Oc, it was a relief to get away, and she soon settled down to her life with the Dwayne clan. Oc drifted off to sleep.

Tat-attan had a deep gash to her forehead and had it dressed by Freya's assistant, Miro, a woman of thirty years, and a friend of Tara's mother, Wayba. Tat was not the typical Wollon woman. She was twenty years old, with three deceased children and the concubine of the chief of the Wollon, Attan-puma. She was one of the chief's favourite women and enjoyed all the benefits that role brought. She was tall and dark-skinned, with a long elongated face, small mouth, bright sparkling eyes and jet black curly hair. She had many bracelets, beautiful necklaces, and a huge array of earrings. Apart from her elongated ears, she had no other piercings. She had resisted her capture but had the intelligence to know that the battle was lost and that it would be prudent for her to go quietly. She did not enjoy the journey back to Dwayne territory on the rafts as she was terrified of water. In the month since her capture, she had done quite well for herself. Tat had taken the eye of the tribe's one-eyed shaman Cleft-tar and had moved to his hearth, to the surprise of all.

Wayba was screaming at Tuan and Ta-nute.

"You did not listen! She is our medicine woman, our prophetess, our witch," pointing as she took a deep breath.

"Do you even remember her name, Freya?"

The old woman looked out from her dark lean-to. She was nearly forty-two, bent from carrying too many heavy loads as a child, her face cracked, weathered and wrinkled. Loose skin was hanging from her body. Her breasts hung down to her waist. She was worn out from too many pregnancies and too many beatings, but her black, piercing eyes blazed with fury. She said in a quiet voice.

"When the earth trembles men should not go to war," "You simply did not listen. Cleft-ta did not listen! You arrogant men, you had to go to war, and now we are being destroyed by the spirits of the dead!"

From inside the lean-to, Freya could be heard chanting a spell.

T wo days after the earthquake, a proliferation of red-hot cinders started to descend from strange dark clouds, obliterating the light from the sun. Forest fires could be seen burning towards the mountains. As the day wore on forest animals screamed and bellowed and terrible darkness descended, and people started to choke on the acrid fumes. Everyone was bewildered. Tuan had to think fast, talking to anyone who would listen he started to bark out orders.

"Get to the river with skins and bladders and collect as much clean water as you can!"

Ta-nute grabbed Tuan.

"Stop! Wait and listen to me! Tell me again that story about your Uncle Uepti when you were seven, and in the mountains with the Tarawa,"

"Not now father, I have too much to do." "Tell me!" Ta-nute pleaded.

Tuan looked into his father's eyes and realised he needed to respond.

"We had climbed to the highest peak and were looking south, it was a clear day, and great birds of prey were circling above so we had to take cover, but Uncle Uepti said that he could see land or maybe it was smoke far away on the horizon. The huge birds flew off towards the South." Tuan's father was touched.

"Tuan, I have to tell you, you are my son, but you have the spirit of the men of the Tarawa. Many years ago, when we were very young, your mother and I had gone to the mountains to trade. I swapped Wayba, who was thirteen, for some good flint blades, and she spent many days with four Tarawa men."

Ta-nute faced Tuan, and holding his head with both hands and with tears streaming down his face. He exclaimed,

"Tuan! My son go! Take the young people of our clan on the bamboo rafts and sail south to the land of the giant birds. The old hag Freya is right, this place is doomed, our totem and the spirits of the forest have been defeated by darkness fire and brimstone."

When Tara was eleven she was a beautiful and intelligent child, full of laughter and fun; she was slim and athletic, and loved by everyone. She was quite tall for her age, with beautiful long legs and black hair. She knew her menstruation would start someday but was still surprised when it happened. It started when she and some other women were collecting mussels at the estuary. They told her that her father would deflower her as was the custom of the Dwayne. Three days later Ta-nute and Cleft-tar had taken her to a quiet place by the river on a hot sultry night. The woman of the clan gently pinned her down on a soft patch of grass and forced open her legs. With other members of the Ta-nute clan watching Ta-nute and Cleft-ta had their way with her. She did not enjoy the experience, she had been torn and was bleeding again. Wayba and Freya looked after her. A number of days passed before she was able to join the other woman. Her childhood was over.

Months later she gave birth to a boy, but it was stunted and deformed. She never saw it. Wayba cut its cord with a sharp flint knife and with some other woman took the little screaming infant to a secluded part of the beach between shallow sand dunes. She found a large rock and kneeling over the tiny child brought the rock down smashing its skull. The other women walked to the tree line and gathered sweet herbs and broad leaves in which to wrap the body. They then found a small hollow log where they placed the tiny wrapped-up body and buried the coffin. The women performed the rites of the dead, singing and wailing to the gods and spirits of fate.

Tuan knew that his father was right. They needed to escape the desolation of their island home. However, Tuan doubted that the tribe's small bamboo rafts would be able to withstand the rigours of an extended passage on the open sea. Meanwhile, Wurk and his people were trying frantically to put out fires that had started in the forest near their area of the camp. The great black cloud was still raining down hot embers and a putrid smell permeated the camp. Occasionally, a ray of sunshine would pierce the gloom revealing a scene of devastation. Tuan took Wurk aside and asked,

"Would you and your clan come with the Tar-nute to the land of the huge birds to the land that must be to the south?"

"That would be impossible as the old witch Freya has put an evil spell on all of us," Wurk replied.

Tuan then thought for a moment and replied,

"But it could be done? We would have to build much larger rafts made from the tallest bamboo shafts and make the smaller rafts seaworthy."

Wurk responded by gyrating and throwing his arms in the air in the customary war dance of the Dewayne. After several minutes, he ran to his hut and selecting a spear sped off to Freya's lean-to. She was standing outside. With one mighty turn of his body, he threw the spear forcibly into the air towards the medicine woman. In a split second it pierced the old woman's chest. For a few moments, she writhed in agony in the dirt and then died. Then Wurk cried out with all his power.

"All of the tribe of the Dwayne, now the past is over and our gods and spirits are dying, we go to the land of the south, to the land of the huge black birds!"

Sahul

The days that followed were harrowing ones for the tribe following the earthquake, tsunami, darkness and fire. Cremations had to take place following the rituals of the Dwayne. Wakes were held for those missing. Tara's father, Ta-nute had been rescued from the river and the entire Ta-nute clan were in mourning for Vashna and the other women who had been washed out to sea. Later things got worse when a massive dark cloud spewing ash and fire blocked the light of the sun. The forest was covered in a thick layer of ash. Fires broke out destroying and suffocating the wonderful plants, and animals. Monsoon rains washed the ash into streams, rivers, and oceans. However, life went on for the tribe, because many were determined to build the rafts and sail south.

How many days had passed, was difficult to say but some semblance of order had now descended on the tribe. The great cloud dissipated slowly. Wurk and Tuan were their leaders, and they now had a plan. Coconuts, edible roots, tubas, and fruits were gathered by the women from the burning forest. Tuan was designing new sea-going rafts with Lay and Parpi, and many able-bodied men were cutting down the very largest bamboo stems and hauling them to the estuary. Soon there would be enough to start construction of the great rafts that would take them to another world.

Tuan had enlisted Lay and Parpi to build the rafts. These men had used similar vessels for fishing, and the larger ones for catching turtles. Tuan had tried to work out how many people would want to make this dangerous voyage of discovery and decided that about fifty would be the likely number. The design of the tribe's rafts differed considerably, but the four larger ones could take four people, so he decided they could use these if they were strengthened by extra strap-down cross beams.

Tuan decided that they would need to build at least four very large rafts to accommodate at least ten people. The problem was that this would be very labour-intensive and they were running out of time. Although the dark cloud of smoke and ash had dispersed, due to strong easterly winds, food supplies were diminishing as the men could no longer hunt while they were working on harvesting the very long bamboo shafts, and constructing the rafts.

Ili, Dor, and Arra were men of the Tarawa and were flint nappers. They had followed the river down from the mountains through the burning and ravaged forest to the camp of the Dwayne. They then reached the estuary where they found Tuan, Lay, Parpi and several women, who were splitting long lengths of vine to use as rope and strapping. They embraced. Tuan,

"We have come in the hope that we could travel south. We know there is land there," said Ili.

"You are welcome," they all exclaimed in the Tarawa tongue.

"Have you brought food?"

"Can you help us make rafts?"

"Where are your women?" There were so many questions.

Yes, they could help them make rafts. Ili explained that they would make flint axes and knives hafted onto wooden handles or embedded in short curved branches, they would set about making them at once. But first, they needed good flint. So Dor and Arra re-traced their steps and found many good flint cores in the river bed, and Tuan watched with rapt attention as the flint nappers set to work. First, they found hammer stones in the river bed. When these had been selected, they took a careful assessment of the larger flint cores and then each one proceeded to take precise aim, striking the core of flint with the hammer stone in such a way as to produce the tools that were required. Thick sharp flakes would be used for axes, and thinner flakes with straight edges for knives and scrapers. The smaller flakes were used for inserting into thin slices of hardwood to make augers and spear tips. Tuan agreed to help them in their work whenever time permitted.

Tuan instinctively knew that the problems of the design of the rafts centred around buoyancy. The design needed to ensure the deck was sufficiently raised above the water to protect the raft from the impact of waves. He discussed the design with Lay and Parpi.

"It could be done by curving the sides of the rafts upwards," Lay suggested.

"And the rafts will need a mast and sail, a weatherproof hut, and a strong pivot point for a steering oar," added Parpi.

After more deliberation, a design was agreed on. The rafts would consist of huge lengths of bamboo stalks arranged flat in three layers and held in place by cross members. The top layer would have curved sides tapering to a point in the front with a projecting pole to serve as guy rope anchors. The bamboo stalks would be tied to thwart timbers by rattan forest vines and straps. There would be an 'A' frame mast for a sail and one or more huts for sleeping and cooking. Tuan was perplexed by the very labour-intensive way the traditional rafts had been built using intricate weaving with vine rope to tie the bamboo stems together. He had to find a quicker way. Tuan spoke to Ili,

"My friend of the mountains," he began,

"Could you make me tools for cutting holes into the sides of the bamboo?" Ili screwed up his weather-beaten face and stroked his short grey beard.

"Let me talk with Dor and Arra," he said.

And so it was done. The flint nappers making small sharp hatchets, perfect for cutting the holes in the side of the bamboo shafts that Tuan needed. Tuan's idea was to cut holes through the bamboo stalks and then drive some green pegs coated with tree resin through the holes for extra strength and speed of construction.

After days of toil, Tuan and Tara needed to talk and rest, so one night Tuan and Tara left the camp and went to a small cave in the cliffs to the east of the estuary. They got themselves comfortable; Tara made a bed by putting a layer of dead leaves and soft foliage on a layer of cold ash to repel ants and bugs. Tara put six-month-old Payu to bed and then lay down next to him. Tara was anxious about Payu, could he make the journey with them on the raft? She spoke to Tuan about her anxiety. He held her gently in his arms,

"I've been thinking about this too," he said,

"If we were to take him it would mean travelling on one of the larger rafts where people could assist us with the baby."

She thought about this for some time. Eventually, she spoke.

"No," she said,

"It would be best if I left Payu with mother and father, that way we can travel on one of the smaller rafts and I could feed you with my milk," she exclaimed. He kissed her passionately and they made love.

"I love you so much," he told her softly.

"My darling brother, I will follow you wherever you may go," she exclaimed.

"But what about Payu?" he asked.

"Don't worry," she laughed, "Mother will find a good wet nurse for him I'm sure."

They woke to the eerie darkness which was so disturbing. It must be evil spirits returning from the dead, thought Tuan. Payu was nursing at his mother's breast. It was dawn but the dense black cloud obscured most of the sunlight. The sunrise was trying to break through the putrid atmosphere. Tuan made a fire on the beach to cook some dead fish and birds that Tara had found for breakfast.

"After breakfast, I shall start organising the men,"

he said, gulping down some fish and grubs.

"I shall look after Payu with Oc today, and organise food for all the Dwayne working on the rafts." She called out after him as he strode off on his long lanky legs towards the estuary.

After about a month into the construction of the rafts, Tuan was pleased with the progress. Thankfully, the black cloud had been largely dispersed by some strong south-easterly winds. Many huge bamboo stems had been laid out in three layers as the base for each raft, with the final layer curving up at the sides with a long projecting pole at the front. The bamboo lengths were collectively lashed together with full rattan vines. Crossbeams were then put in place at regular intervals with the men from the Tarawa cutting holes through the cross beams and into the bamboo base. As instructed by Tuan, other men and boys were cutting and fashioning green pegs coated with resin to drive through the holes in the cross beams and into the base, locking it all together. The women, who had made the long lengths of strapping had also been weaving it between the huge logs

of bamboo for extra strength. The next stage would involve fitting the 'A' frame masts and weather-proof huts.

When the sun was high in the sky and the men and women had stopped work, Tara, Oc, and many boys and girls delivered food to the workers. Suddenly there was a warning cry from the western side of the estuary, it was Brun, who was running at top speed towards them screaming something.

"What is he saying? What is he saying? What's going on?" said Tuan.

Someone shouted,

"It's the Wollon. There are Wollon spearmen on the western beach!"

They were all stunned because that was thought to be impossible. There was no way that the Wollon could be there as they had no rafts to sail around the high headland. The rugged terrain and high cliffs of the headland making it impassable for all. The tide was coming in and the huge tethered rafts were beginning to lift off.

"All of you stay where you are," Tuan said, and without hesitation ran to the river and dived into the brackish water. He swam about ten metres to the western bank where Brun pulled him from the water and pointed down the beach.

"There they are," he said,

Tuan saw three Wollon spearmen in full war attire, their brown bodies painted black, with white zig-zag stripes on their bodies and arms. They carried spears and shields. The group was slowly walking down the beach towards them. Tuan could also see another small group of people behind them. He pointed towards the camp,

"Brun run to the camp as fast as you can, find Wurk and get him to come at once with three good men with spears; go now as fast as you can, and remember to say, only three men."

Soon Wurk came running towards them down the slope and onto the beach with three men carrying spears. Wurk came up to Tuan and looked down the beach towards the fast-approaching Wollons. Wurk quickly assessed the situation. Standing by Tuan's side Wurk gestured to the approaching party and asked, "What do you make of it?" "It's not a war party, that's all I know for sure," replied Tuan.

The two men standing together on the beach made a considerable contrast. Wurk was twenty-two, stocky with broad powerful shoulders and legs, and a brown muscular body, long black hair, hung loosely about his shoulders. His small deep-set eyes portrayed a high intelligence. Tuan, however, was tall and of medium build, with a light brown body. The men were comrades, and they respected each other's judgement and trusted each other fully. They steadfastly waited for the Wollon.

The three Wollon warriors stopped some distance from the two men. Two women and four children slowly emerged from behind them. Tuan could see that the women and children were restrained with leads held by the warriors and attached to collars placed around their necks. They all looked exhausted. At a sharp command, the women and children prostrated themselves on the ground. The warriors then suddenly discarded their spears and shields, casting them to the ground. Tuan and Wurk stood there bemused. The problem was that Tuan had only a very rudimentary understanding of the Wollon language. Tuan asked, "What do you want?" complete with a shrug of his shoulders and hands in the air.

One of the men on the right-hand side of the group said one word, "Tat-attan." Tuan and Wurk looked at each other, they understood. Attan-puma wanted his woman back.

Time passed. Neither group would give ground. They stood in silence, waiting. But Tuan saw that the tide was coming in and the heat was unbearable. He also realised that the women and children were in considerable distress. They could not stay where they were on the beach. People in the camp were alert to possible danger and had congregated on the tree line to watch. Wurk barked an order to Brun, who had been standing nearby.

"Go and fetch Tat."

Tuan beckoned the tribes-people on the tree line to back away and motioned the Wollon warriors to follow him. They picked up their spears and shields and tugging sharply on the leads of the women and children, they slowly made their way up to an open area of tufted grass in the shade between some trees that had not been covered in ash. Some women came and gave the children water in wooden cups. Three of the children were crying, but another, the eldest girl, just looked on, defiant. She fixed her gaze on Tuan and pointed to her mouth. Some boys and girls from the crowd came over with food. The Wollon's were famished and greedily accepted the gifts of food and drink. The tension between the two groups lessened and the Wollon warriors looked across the estuary and saw the raft-building operation in full swing. They stared in amazement as the huge stems of bamboo were carried into place. With meany women lashing them into position with vines on the now floating rafts. Brun returned and announced,

"Tat won't come, and she won't go back to Attan-puma because he has bad teeth."

Under his breath, Tuan swore an oath to the gods of thunder and lightning. He looked at Wurk, and with a shrug of his shoulders murmured.

"Now what?"

Wurk barked an order to Brun,

"Go and fetch Oc!"

Tuan nodded his approval, and Brun ran off on his errand. Tuan now gestured to the onlookers to go and get on with their work. They all departed back to the camp.

Now Tuan had time to closely observe the women and children. The two women were both medium height and would be middle-aged, about thirty. Like the men and children, they were naked with slightly sagging bodies and breasts, their greyish hair short and frizzy. They were much adorned with trinkets, bone necklaces and bracelets. They kept their heads bowed and looked resigned to their fate, whatever that might be. The four children, two boys and two girls had badly scratched arms and legs. The boys standing to the left were about five or six years old and sobbing. The first girl on the right seemed slow-witted. The last girl standing to the right of the group was about ten. She was quite fat, with a pleasant round face and a small nose which was wide at the nostrils. She had a light brown body with the first indications of breasts. She joined the middle finger and thumb of her right hand together to make a circle and thrust her middle finger through it several times. The meaning of the gesture was unmistakable. Tuan replied with a gesture of his own, his index fingers in the form of a cross. She screwed up her face and stuck her tongue out at him. The precocious devil he thought, and she has probably not yet come of age. He knew that it was very bad for a girl to be mated with men when too young. The fat girl made a forceful chewing gesture with her mouth and pointed a finger at herself. Did he want to eat her?

Once again he formed a cross with his fingers. She thought for a moment then put the middle finger of her left hand in her mouth and sucked. She looked at him with expectation.

Once again, he made the cross with his fingers. She looked at Tuan, shrugged her shoulders and gestured as if to say, well, what do you want?

Brun arrived somewhat out of breath and announced,

"Oc will not come, she said she will not go near any Wollon men."

What trouble they were in, with no interpreter. However, at that moment Tara arrived. She was dripping wet having swum across the river. Throwing an arm around Tuan's shoulder and giving him a gorgeous smile, she kissed him on the cheek.

"I have learnt some of their language from Oc, would you like me to help?"

Tuan gestured towards the Wollon warriors. Then Tara pointed at the women and children,

"What are these for?" she asked.

The warriors conferred with one another, and then one spoke.

"I believe they say that they are presents from Attan-puma and that we can eat them, or use them as slaves if we like, they are for the return of Tat."

Wurk was angry and replied,

"Tat-attan is our captive, she will stay with us, go home."

And he pointed towards the west. The Wollon men understood immediately and threw away their weapons. They then pushed the women and children down onto the ground between the high tufts of grass and prostrated themselves. Tuan thought, what use are they to us two useless women and two useless young boys, a backward girl and another that only thinks of sex?

He called out to them and gestured for them to rise. He pointed to them and then to the rafts. The Wollon warriors looked at each other then gave a great shout of joy and threw their arms in the air. They would come with them on the rafts to the south, to the land of the huge black birds. Wurk came up to Tuan and slapped him on the back and laughed and laughed and laughed.

Calm brown seawater lapped with little ripples near where they stood. In the evening, the tide would turn, and by morning the Dwayne women would begin collecting worms and maggots from the rotting fish on the beach, as food was becoming increasingly hard to find. The tribe was resigned to eating ants, stinkbugs, earwigs, maggots and any edible fungi that proliferated in the hot and humid conditions.

Over the next few days, the campsite by the estuary was swept and cleared of ash and debris. Tat-attan was determined to stay with Cleft-tar, who swore she would never go near the water and rafts again. Tar-nute and Wayba would also stay. They offered to look after Payu while they were gone. Most of the older people of the tribe decided to stay. Zika said she wanted to go and would take Osto. The Odaa-nas clan would also join them. Oc was happy to go with the Tar-nute clan, providing she would not be travelling with any Wollon men. Then there were Ili, Dor and Arra, who were still hoping that some of the Tarawa women would make it to the estuary. Finally, they needed to make room for the Wollon group of nine tribespeople.

The weather was oppressive, with occasional thunder and electric storms, with the sea rough one minute, and calm the next. Final preparations were underway with some people already saying goodbye to their extended families and friends. At the estuary, Tuan, Tobo, and Boni were working on the rafts. It was still quite early in the day when there was a shout, it was Tobo pointing in an easterly direction along the coast. Much to the amazement of the men a fleet of canoes could be seen slowly making their way towards them. Tuan counted six canoes. Shortly, the canoes were beached at the estuary, and the occupants lay exhausted on the blackened mudflats. A crowd of onlookers had gathered to see who it could possibly be. There were shouts of delight when it was realised that three of the women were of the Tarawa tribe, and the women of Ili, Dor, and Arra.

The far east of the island was the territory of a small tribe named the Berri-jaa. They were lakeside people who used canoes for fishing on a great lake. The Tarawa women, Suuti, Mia, and Kirra had travelled over high mountain passes to avoid the chaos and devastation of the forest. They sought the territory of the Berri-jaa, where they hoped to reach the land of the Dwayne.

They arrived at a time of anguish for the tribe of the Berri-jaa, for death and destruction from the earthquake had left the people fearful and angry. The Tarawa women explained that the forest was now impassable. They said that their men had decided to follow the streams and creeks down to the estuary and the land of the Dwayne, in the hope of travelling south. They were given a warm welcome by the shaman, Dreg, and a place to rest. He told them that the tribe would help them travel to the territory of the Dwayne, once the spirits of their tribe had been appeased.

Two days later, Suuti, Mia, and Kirra joined the remnants of the tribe to watch the surviving men of the Berri-jaa dancing a ritual dance to the spirits of the tribe and lake. They did not understand why their land had been so devastated by fire and ash, and why so many of their people had fallen sick and died. What had they done wrong? Were the spirits angry with them, and how could they be appeased?

The dance was the dance of sacrifice. At the end of the dance, a young girl is chosen to be sacrificed to the spirits and gods of the lake by drowning. She would be tightly bound and thrown into the lake. All the women and girls were petrified. The rhythmic dance was slowly coming to its terrifying conclusion, in a crescendo of drums, shouts and a swirl of arms, legs and billowing dust. The dancers stopped. All was silent. The women of the Tarawa watched in horror as a young girl was chosen. It was Neti, an orphan girl, eight years old, and a virgin. She was bound and carried to the lake writhing and kicking in a desperate effort to escape, but all to no avail.

A storm was approaching. Thunder and lightning rolled and crashed across the darkening sky. A black shadow cast an ominous spell across the black and sombre lake. It appeared to be moving at great speed. Then, accompanied by the noise of a rushing wind, the huge bird plummeted from the thunderous sky. It came falling, gyrating and screaming from above. They all looked on in amazement as the giant bird smashed into the lake before them, causing a fountain of spray and broken wings.

The men and women of the Berri-jaa understood this strange event as a sign from the totem spirits. A very good omen. But they needed to respect the message from the gods and act wisely. Now the pressing question was how to get the Tarawa women safely to the Dwayne. Dreg called for volunteers.

"Brave men and women of the Berri-jaa, who will paddle along the coast to the territory of the Dwayne in our canoes?"

Then it was decided. Neti was adopted by the Tarawa women. They with six men and three women of the Berri-jaa; would cut and drag their canoes through the well-known tracks of their rainforest home to the south coast, and in an epic journey, the six canoes would travel west along the coast to the estuary of the Dwayne.

Now Tuan was faced with a major logistical problem. He had too many people and not enough rafts. He did a headcount. The Ta-nute clan included twenty-five plus himself and Tara. Adding the volunteers together from the various tribes, he recognised seventy-nine courageous men, women and, children had trusted him to lead this perilous journey. That evening, Tuan held a conference with Wurk, Lay, Parpi, Ili, and Tobo, the main men responsible for the construction of the rafts. He explained the situation.

"I believe we should take all those who wish to go, do you all agree?" They all agreed.

"I also believe it imperative that the people on the rafts should stay together on this journey, they will need to be taught how to sail, do you all agree?" That too was accepted.

"So how can we do it? I'm asking for advice," said Tuan. The four big rafts may be able to take twelve if we reduce the stores to maybe forty-eight people. With luck, we may be able to get five on the four smaller reinforced rafts, if two of them are children. That means we still need to accommodate eleven more people, and time is running out as the food situation is now desperate."

"We simply need to build another large raft," suggested Tobo.

"Not possible, we don't have any more long bamboo shafts," said Parpi.

Tuan looked around for inspiration.

"Any suggestions Lay?" he asked.

"Simple," said Lay.

"We have many shorter lengths of bamboo already cut and unused, and plenty of pegs that we did not need. I think we could make use of these to make three more small rafts, which would hold about three or four people."

"Brilliant, Lay," Tuan replied.

"I think we should get on with it as the moon is starting to wax. If we can be ready in two weeks we will have the full moon." And so it was agreed.

The following morning, Tuan announced that there would be a delay because more small sea-going rafts would need to be built. The whole camp and estuary became a hive of activity. Some of women were making sails woven from palm leaf, and others created containers for storing food made from hollow mangrove logs. Other women had found thin bamboo stems to line the hut frames, all scavenged from the forest. They were busy fitting these stems to the strong weatherproof huts. Children had woven sun hats from reeds and fibre and shaped buckets from large folded leaves and resin. The six men of the Berri-jaa shaped wooden steering oars and bamboo paddles and masts, carefully rounding off any rough edges of the sharp bamboo. Dor and Arra provided an assortment of fine craft maintenance tools, including knife blades, axe heads and scrapers.

The Wollon were taking up too much of Tuan's time because they were having a great deal of difficulty adjusting to the culture of the Dwayne. There had been fights among the three Wollon spearmen over women. The Wollon men were hated by everyone. Tuan was criticised for allowing them to come without any consultation. It was not just the culture that caused problems, but also the language. Strangely, the men did not appear to have names. Tuan felt that his instinct to take them was the right course of action, however, he decided to talk the matter over with Tara that night.

They had a good meal of slow roast scorpions with the stingers removed of course, and Payu was quiet and happily sucking on pebbles, supervised by Oc.

"My beautiful brother, some things are just best for women to work out, would you like me to make a suggestion?" she offered, but without waiting for a reply she continued.

"Let's give them all names, Oc any suggestions?" She called out. But Oc was busy holding the baby by its ankles and giving it a wack on its back to dislodge a stone that it was choking on. She gave it another sharp wack and instantaneously Payu gave a choking sound, then a cough and ejected the stone. Oc replied, with a mix of gestures and some words she had learned.

"Wollon people not always have name. I have always been known as Oc. Men will not tell you their name, or totem, men of tribe would know only. The women's names removed because their men dead," she shrugged her shoulders.

She took a deep breath and went on.

"Children have name but shy to tell."

"Shall we leave it for tomorrow?" said Tuan, hopefully.

"We will get them all together and give them names tomorrow," said Tara.

They put Payu down and all snuggled up together on the nice comfortable sleeping area that Tara had made. Tara and Tuan made love and went to sleep. Later that night, Oc snuggled up to Tara but could not sleep. She loved that beautiful woman so much for accepting her so completely. She just lay there gazing at her in the moonlight. A little later Tara woke and gave Oc one of her breasts to suck, then they drifted into a blissful sleep.

In the morning, Tuan started sailing lessons, as Lay and Parpi were busy. Two of the large rafts had been fitted with masts and sails. Tuan began with the key skills of sailing, such as running before the wind, tacking, and going about. He then demonstrated how to raise the sail to the top of the mast without damage. Most of the Berri-jaa were on the first raft and were very happy and excited to learn; although they were highly adept at manoeuvring canoes they had never used sails. Kirra of the Tarawa was with them to interpret his instructions, given she knew their language. Members of the Odaa-nas clan, including Wurk, were on the second raft and had no difficulty working out what to do. They had used small rafts with sails all their lives but knew it would be a challenge sailing these huge rafts with much larger sails.

Meanwhile, Tara and Oc had rounded up the Wollon people. They brought them down to the estuary where they all stood watching the sailing lessons, pointing and jabbering excitedly amongst themselves about the frenetic activity of the boat-building operation. Tuan joined them and gesturing towards Oc said,

"Could you ask them their names?"

Oc gathered the children together and bent down low, speaking to them quietly and with a happy countenance. The boys giggled.

"Their names are Ap and Zon. Oc bent down and spoke to the girls.

"The girls called Slow and Fat," she said.

And then, as an afterthought,

"Women would like you give them names."

"What about the men?" said Tara.

"They will never tell," said Oc. With a vigorous shaking of the head and a shrug of the shoulders.

But what of the adult women? The two Wollon women looked on but said nothing. They were middle-aged and nondescript women, with greying hair and sagging breasts. They both wore unattractive beads and trinkets. What to call them? Tuan could not work it out. He said to Oc,

"Ask them what they like to do."

Oc complied. The two women turned and faced each other then they gently put their arms around each other and in a very touching way embraced. "Who would know what trials and tribulations, heartache, and pain they have endured throughout their lives," thought Tuan.

Tara was bewildered by her brother's focus on the women. Why is he wasting his valuable time on these people, they have been our enemies for as long as I can remember, she wondered.

Then Tuan decided,

"I name the two women Spirit, and Hope, the two girls names shall remain Slow and Fat until they can prove themselves useful. The men,

I name the one with big ears, Ears, the tallest man Tree and the man with the great scar on his face, Scar," Tuan continued.

"Now Oc, please ask if they have definitely decided to come with us on the rafts, and how they got onto the western beach."

Oc consulted,

"Yes, they will all come. Down rope from high cliff. Faith and Hope, say Wurk killed their men, now want to be slaves of Wurk."

Tuan called Wurk over and explained what had happened.

"I would like to split the men up."

"They are good strong men, I'll grant you that," said Wurk.

"We could put each one of them on the steering oars at the back of the big rafts. That would keep them out of the way," Wurk continued.

"I'll have the women and get them cleaning. What you do with the children is your concern," he said, walking off.

Tara was with her mother, Wayba. They were crying.

"In a few more days you will be fifteen years old," she said.

"Mother I want you to have Payu, I'm sure you will be able to find a wet nurse to feed him, he is too young to survive the journey on the rafts,"

"I will look after him until you return, I promise, and come back to say goodbye to your father," said Wayba.

The last of the stores were being loaded. Hollow mangrove logs had been filled with drinking water and sealed with wood and beeswax. Dried fruit, coconuts, honeycomb, baskets of salted meat and fish, had been saved for the voyage. They had also gathered cooking buckets, stone mortar and pestle, alongside fireboxes and bundles of wood. What could go wrong?

It was late afternoon in the camp, and if the weather was good they would be leaving the next day. They made their last farewells. Tara talked briefly to Zika and little Osto to make sure they were prepared and ready to go, and then she felt a tap on her shoulder. She swung round to find Cleft-ta standing behind her. She was surprised as they had always avoided each other. He looked in her eyes,

"I know I did wrong to you many years ago."

He then handed her an exquisitely carved bone comb.

"It's for you," he said. He bowed his head, turned, and walked away.

Tuan, Tara, and Oc had decided to adopt Slow Girl. That evening, she was in their cave helping Tara prepare a meal of crocodile stakes. All being well, that night would be their last night in the cave. But Tuan was not happy. Tara thought he had been a bit moody for the last few days, but had put it down to the pressure he was under. Tara noticed he was rubbing his mouth.

"What's wrong?" she asked.

"Toothache," said Tuan.

"Which one?"

"The front upper tooth to the right," he replied.

"Let's have a look. Oc, could you help me for a moment?"

Oc lifted his upper lip,

"I can't see much it's too dark in here," said Tara,

"Come to the front of the cave, Tuan."

He shuffled toward the cave opening.

"That's better, now we can see. Your gum is very red and swollen... what do you think, Oc?"

"It come out," was her brief reply.

"No, no, just give me something for it," pleaded Tuan.

"Tuan, I don't think that would work, there's an abscess under the tooth. I could try and lance it but the best person to do it would be Miro, but it may take ages to find her." Tuan slumped down holding his mouth,

"Is very painful," he mumbled.

"Poor darling, I know how hard it is to give up a tooth. I'm busy preparing a meal, so just decide what you want to do. I could easily remove it for you but we need to find a long length of sinew. I had plenty of practice drawing teeth from Vashna," she added.

Tuan was very reluctant to have the tooth out, feeling embarrassed and self-conscious to have such a visible tooth removed. But he was in so much pain and he still had so much to do.

"There's sinew in the rafts. I will go and get some," he said.

When he returned, Oc tied one end of the sinew around a small rock at the entrance of the cave, while Tara attached the other end to the tooth.

"Now move back and lay your head back until the sinew is taut," Tara told Tuan.

$$\diamond$$

With a quick jerk, Oc yanked on the cord.

"Ow," cried Tuan.

"Here it is," said Tara, holding up the sinew with Tuan's front tooth dangling from it. Tuan's mouth spouted blood.

Sometime later, Miro arrived with fungus powder and a wad of crocodile skin. She mixed the powder with water. "Drink this Tuan, it will take away the pain," she said. Tuan nodded and swallowed the drink. She then plugged the bleeding hole in Tuan's gum with a small piece of soft crocodile skin and an antiseptic cream made from coconut oil, beeswax, and calendula.

"The drink I gave you is very powerful, it will make you very sleepy indeed, you won't be going anywhere tomorrow," she explained.

Tuan slept late the following morning. Oc had made a fire and brought him warm sweet tea. Tara and Slow Girl were sitting outside of the cave in the morning sun, watching the rafts hoist their sails and set off to the south, on a calm sea, with a light northeast breeze. Tuan's raft still lay at anchor in the estuary.

By midday, Tuan was feeling better as the effect of the drug wore off, although his mouth was still extremely sore. Ta-nute, Wayba, and Payu came down for a last goodbye.

"I have found a good wet nurse, so don't worry about Payu," offered Wayba.

Ta-nute said nothing and seemed self-absorbed and lost in his thoughts. Tuan spoke to Tara and Oc,

"I think I will be fine to go tonight as we have everything we need stored in the raft. It is a fast raft with a good sail so I think we'll be able to catch up with them."

That evening the good weather weather persisted with a light north-easterly breeze. They clambered onto their raft at last. Tuan went to the front and pulled up the anchor. Soon they were underway. Nobody was at the estuary to see them go.

Tuan's raft was constructed of bamboo pontoons, keeping the main deck well clear of the water. It was about three metres wide and four meters in length. At the back, there was the waterproof hut made of a frame of curved bamboo covered with several layers of large woven leaves, it had doors front and back, all protected by tree resin. The sail was held in place at the base with release straps in each corner, with a halyard used to take the sail to the top of the mast. Stores and spare parts were kept in containers in the middle of the raft, tied down with strong straps. Cooking appliances and firewood were kept in the hut.

After Tuan had raised the sail to the top of the mast and secured it, he clambered to the back and took hold of the steering oar. He felt relieved and in control. A huge weight seemed to lift from his shoulders. He had done all he could, now everything was in the hands of the gods and spirits of the tribe. He put a hand to his hair bun and took out a tiny fold of white snakeskin, kissed it, and carefully put it back. Slow Girl was leaning over the side trailing a hand in the water. Oc was in a corner of the hut, feeling very afraid, and curled up in a ball. Tara stood by the mast, and by the last light of the sunset, looked back at her slowly receding island home.

The little group rested comfortably despite the cramped conditions in the hut. Tuan and Tara had taken it in turn to sail the raft during the night. Dawn broke as Tuan took his bearings from the morning star to check that they were still sailing due south. The sea was calm, the only noise was the gentle lapping of the waves in the light breeze. Oc finally came out of the hut and looked around. She was getting used to the raft and the motion of the waves.

"Oc hungry," she announced.

"Seed bread," said Slow Girl in the Wollon tongue, and rubbed her tummy.

"Come help me light up the firebox and prepare the seeds in the mortar and we will soon have a nice breakfast," Oc replied.

The day wore on, the wind freshened and veered to the north. The raft was making good speed running before the wind. For the first time, they were out of sight of land. Tuan was fishing with a harpoon made for him by Arra, but he was having no luck.

"It will be necessary for us to catch fish," he called out to Tara, who was on the steering oar. "Who knows how long our food will have to last."

But just a few minutes later there was a scream from Slow Girl, who had been trailing a small net over the port side,

"Ooh, help! Ooh, help!" she screamed.

Oc was just able to grab her and the net before she went over the side. A beautiful ray-finned fish was thrashing about in the net. Tuan rushed over, speared it and hauled it on board. I was sure she would bring us luck thought Tuan, as he struggled with the creature. The sun was going down and promising a glorious red sunset, but still there was no sign of the other rafts.

Another day dawned, bringing a freshening wind that had gone around to the northwest, causing Tuan to take down the sail to be safe. The sea was rough, water was splashing over the sides, and everything was drenched.

"We will paddle for a bit and watch the weather," said Tuan.

Storm clouds could be seen on the horizon with flashes of lightning. The sea was choppy, the day warm and oppressive. Oc was sick. Slow Girl slipped over and grazed her arm. She screamed and sobbed.

It was about mid-afternoon when they saw another raft in the distance, to the port side. It was one of the large rafts and something was wrong, it had no sail. People on board were frantically waving to them.

"Can you see who they are?"

"I think they are some of the Odaa-nas," said Tara.

"We can't help them, the wind is too high and I can't risk putting up the sail," Tuan explained.

"But we have to do something, we have to!" demanded Tara.

"It's impossible! I will not put our raft at risk," said Tuan.

They continued to watch on helplessly. The wind became westerly which seemed to have the effect of blowing the big raft away from them. They remained watching until it grew dark. When they woke the next day the big raft was nowhere to be seen. The wind had dropped and the sea was calm, there was a light breeze from the northwest.

✦

Tuan put the sail up. The raft was running a broad reach due south and making good speed. It was near midday and the sea had become choppy again, with a freshening breeze. Oc and Slow Girl were cuddled up in the hut having a nap. Tara was steering and Tuan was standing by the mast looking out.

"I think I can see something far away and on the starboard side," he called.

"Is it a raft?" shouted Tara.

She locked the steering oar with a strap and came over to Tuan through the hut, weaving her way past all the stores on the deck. As time passed, it became clear that it was a rocky outcrop sticking out of the sea with waves and foam breaking over it. As they passed by the intrepid seafarers looked in awe at this monolith of green-grey, craggy rock, suggesting a huge finger pointing skyward. It appeared to climb out of the turbulent sea to be enveloped in mist and foam. Sea birds wheeled about overhead. None of them had ever seen anything like it before. It was a timely warning for them to watch out for rocks. In the evening, Tuan caught a strange looking fish with his harpoon, and Oc gutted it and scaled it with a sharp flint knife and scraper. It made a good meal along with Oc's freshly cooked seed bread. After dark, Tuan checked his direction by the Southern Cross and satisfied himself that they were on a true course to the south.

That night, Tuan and Tara would sleep in the hut, while Oc and Slow Girl kept watch; Oc on the steering oar, and Slow Girl tied in with a vine rope, at the front. The night sky was magnificent with a silver moon, shooting stars, and the Milky Way displaying all its majesty.

Tara awoke, and rubbing her eyes, found Tuan lying beside her, his hot sweaty body covered in a wrap. She blew in his ear,

"Darling you need a shave," she said.

He smiled at her, and rolling over embraced her. She was radiant and at that moment they had not a care in the world. She was finding the rocking motion of the raft exceedingly erotic, so she held his penis while he sucked on a breast and drank some of her delicious milk; he let out a sigh and came all over her body, she laughed,

"Now go and have a shave," she said.

He gave in and reached over for his pouch to find one of his sharp shaving shells. Slow Girl came in giggling and brought them some breakfast of salt meat, some leftover seed bread, coconut, and honeycomb. Tuan said to Tara,

"She has done well, hasn't she?" said Tuan.

"She still makes a lot of mistakes. Remember the time she put beeswax in her hair to try and straighten it out?" Tara replied. They both laughed.

It was mid-afternoon, and Tuan had taken the steering oar. The wind had changed again so Tara was setting the sail for the starboard reach when Oc cried out, "Rafts! Land!" And to their amazement, off the port bow and away in the distance, there was a line of rafts. Three large rafts could be seen and some of the smaller ones. They were moored on the lee side of a low volcanic island, in a chain of small islands stretching away to the east. All the islands were low and barren providing an ideal nesting ground for gulls and terns.

"I'm sure we can get over to them," Tuan called out.

"We'll stay on this reach for a while, then I'll go about."

Tara understood exactly what he was going to do.

They sailed on with a feeling of excitement and expectation. Within a couple of hours, Tuan put the raft about and arrived alongside the mooring of the first large raft. Tuan could see that it was moored by a rope attached to the rock face of the island. The people were all resting and sunbathing on a nice smooth sloping area of volcanic rock, well away from the noisy, squawking birds. They were all naked except for their sun hats. They waved. They were the Tarawa men and women. Tuan called out in the Tarawa tongue,

"What are you doing?"

"We are having a rest and some are repairing damage sustained in the storm," Dor replied. Tuan asked, "What happened to the other raft?" Ili shook his head.

"We think they had somebody overboard. Then we saw their sail blow away."

"Apart from that, we have all kept together well," Dor chipped in.

"We have all decided to rest here for another two days before going on."

"Do you have enough water?" asked Tuan.

"Yes, there's plenty in rock pools on these islands and nice big crabs."

"What about Lay, Parpi, and Brun," shouted Tuan.

"They're alright," came a reply from one of the Tarawa women.

"They are exploring some of the other islands."

Slow Girl and Neti were waving at each other fervently. Tuan, Tara, Oc, and Slow Girl got together in a huddle.

"We go! No need stay here on barren island," said Oc, with a flurry of gestures.

"We are going, good luck," said Tuan finally.

Slow Girl waved. They hoisted the sail, swung the raft around, and soon were on their way south through a gap in the island chain. They had not even bothered to put a foot on land.

And so another day dawned. The sea was choppy with overcast cloud, thunder and periods of rain. The wind was fresh from the north, they were making good speed. Gulls wheeled overhead, and turns dived headlong into the ocean for fish. After breakfast, Slow Girl was in her favourite position at the front watching out for rocks, Tara was steering. Tuan decided to try and talk to Oc, as he was starting to understand some of the Wollon language. Tuan turned to Oc, "I'm pleased with Slow Girl," he managed to say, gesturing towards the young Wollon girl.

"She tries very hard, and she always does the best she can. I would like to give her a better Name."

Oc gave him a wonderful smile, "Ask," she said, pointing to the front of the raft.

At that moment, there was a scream from Slow Girl, "Rock! Rock!" Pandemonium broke out on the raft as Tara instinctively threw the steering oar to the right to swing the raft to the port side. Oc slipped and fell. Then the sail fell on Tuan. For a moment he could not move. He then scrambled out from under the crumbled, heavy sail. He reached the front of the raft and gasped,

"Where are the rocks?"

Slow Girl pointed, and he threw up his hands in relief.

"They are not rocks," he said.

"They are Dolphins."

He held her in his arms and whispered in her ear,

"Would you like a better name, you deserve it?" he asked.

She pushed back and looked at him, then kissed him on the cheek. She looked at him very seriously,

"No!" she responded in perfect Dwayne,

"Me, Slow Girl."

It would take some time to get things in order. They were adrift in the choppy water. Tara was helping Oc, who had grazed and bruised her buttocks. Tuan had at last found the spare sail in the stores, but to make matters increasingly difficult the sea was getting rough with a slow-rolling swell. The raft was no longer under control, and Tuan was tired and confounded. He still had to fit the halyard to the new sail but that was proving difficult. The raft was heaving and pitching. He lost his balance and slipped; waves were crashing over the bow in sheets of spray. He just sat on the deck with his head in his hands. He started to cry. Tara and Oc got him into the hut. It was getting dark and starting to rain. They closed the doors and all huddled in the hut as the raft rose, fell, and twisted in the swell. Whitecaps broke over the sides of the raft. The raft was drenched by waves, wind, and rain. They were all hungry and wet, but it was impossible to eat. They spent a miserable, starless night, being tossed about, fearful and afraid.

Oc woke in the middle of the night from a fitful sleep. She felt sick and reached over the side of the raft. Sometimes, the moon would peek through a break in the clouds. She thought she could see something on the horizon when the raft was on the peak of a wave, but she was not sure. She went back into the hut and cuddled up to the others.

✦

Tara woke with sunlight in her eyes. She blinked, wondering where she was. Then she realised that sunlight was coming in through some holes in the side of the hut, punctured by the wind in the night. She looked out of the doorway and could see the others standing on the deck, and looking out to sea. She thought Tuan hasn't got the new sail up yet. Tuan turned around and saw that she was awake. He stretched his left arm through the doorway and offered her his hand. She took it and stood beside him. Without saying a word Tuan waved his arm across the horizon. Tara let out a gasp at a magnificent vista of land stretching from east to west, as far as the eye could see. Slow Girl looked at Tara, then grabbed Tara's hands and jumped up and down excitedly, screaming her head off.

Tuan didn't bother replacing the sail as a brisk north wind was relentlessly blowing them south, and if it held Tuan thought they would make landfall sometime that afternoon. Tara and Oc stood on the deck, hand in hand looking at the vastness of the fateful shore slowly revealing itself.

"No mountain, all flat," said Oc.

By midday, they could see much more, dunes stretching in both directions and birds of many types in great profusion. They could see flamingos, storks and gulls, with raptors soaring high above.

"Please start paddling, watch out for reefs and shallows, and be prepared to fend off or swim if the raft gets grounded," Tuan bellowed with much excitement.

But the wind was dropping, there wasn't a cloud in the sky and the sea was almost flat. They all started to paddle, including Slow Girl, as best she could. But would they ever get there?

Tara could see the beach and dunes more clearly now, and it was obvious that the beach was littered with debris of all kinds. Their excitement knew no bounds.

"Oc no swim," shouted Oc.

And then they ran aground on a sandbank some way from the beach and stuck fast. The tide was going out. Tara could not wait, she jumped into the warm water from the front of the raft and waded a short distance. Then, when the water was deep enough, she swam as fast as she could to the shore, putting her feet down on soft, smooth sand. She then slowly and carefully climbed onto the beach.

It was late in the day, and the shadows threw into contrast the mounds and ripples of the dunes sculpted by wind and rain. Tara raised her head, and looking up to the crest of the dune wondered what lay beyond.

By our reckoning, the time was 5:20 pm on Tuesday the 23rd of March 70,069 BP (before the present). Tara Ta-nute was the first homo sapien to set foot on the continent of Sahul. She was the first Australian.

Sahul
Part 2

Foreword

M any thousands of years after the first human footprint appeared on an Australian beach (Sahul) the climate changed. The world was warming up. The huge polar ice caps were melting, and sea levels were rising.

Many bands, descendants of the first settlers now long forgotten, sought safety from the rising waters. Some bands travelled east, while others travelled west along the northern coast. Smaller numbers headed inland through the marshes in search of a place of refuge.

A young boy and his mother set out on a journey to escape the rising waters. Through inhospitable and unyielding landscapes, the home of Megafauna, rival tribes, and conflicting spirits, the boy discovers his power to lead his band to the centre of a continent and beyond, to the ultimate destination, and finally, to the discovery of his conscience.

Sahul-Part Two

✧

He could remember the dream about shooting stars in the night sky, of milk, a terrible face and waking up screaming. On her back, he held tight around his mother's neck. Fingers tightly entwined in the mass of her mop of tangled hair. His legs gripped her waist. She was naked except for a thin belt of woven reed that held a small pouch containing white ochre. The going was difficult. The weather was overcast, warm, and humid.

Noname was tipped one way, and then with a jolt was flung in the other direction, as his mother jumped, swayed and navigated carefully across undulating rocks. The rain was heavy. Water ran down his face and into his eyes. The smell of Noname's mother was comforting as he licked the sweat from her neck. She had walked all day, clambering over rocks and jumping over fast-flowing creeks. She stopped to catch her breath and to survey the land holding her hands to her brow to shield her eyes from the rain. She needed to eat and find shelter. In the distance, she could see the faint outline of some low grey hills, but she would not get there today, she had come to an impasse. A wide river. She put the toddler down in a patch of mud. He squealed with delight happy to be off his mother's back. She got to work building a temporary shelter from brushwood, utilising weathered bark and wide thick leaves tied together with vine.

As his mother laboured, Noname had scratched about on all fours looking for something to eat. He had dug down with a stick to reveal some fat, ripe tubers, but was unable to extract them from the brown, sticky mud. He screamed in frustration.

Although tired and hungry, his mother came to him and kneeling beside him put him on her breast. She sang a song "Hoia-ho, hoia-ho, wigimajara' repeated time and time again. Noname had found some soft crawling creatures on broad leaves. The woman smiled at her clever three-year-old, as he reached out to her with a handful of huge soft, slimy slugs. She immediately devoured them with relish. She then picked him up, and wiping off the mud from his naked body took him inside the shelter.

It was late in the day, and the rain had stopped. The night was falling. Then the soothing sound of the flowing river as mother and son snuggled down together, their body warmth comforting against the chill of the evening air. Mother slowly chewed on the fat tubers found earlier, softening them and pressing them into his mouth. There was no wind. All was calm. Tomorrow, she would have to find a way to cross the river. She would need the ancestor's guidance to fulfil her compulsive and uncontrollable desire to travel south away from the inundation of her homeland.

She awoke to the sound of birdsong and the rushing river with the sunrise. She felt the excitement of a new day. Her people would eventually follow them she was sure. Maybe today. She stepped out of the shelter carrying the still-sleeping child. She was confident in the power of the spirit world to guide them on their way.

The mother walked down to the river hand in hand with Noname. Sunlight flashed off the rapidly flowing current, and eddies slowly swirled and bubbled over rocks and debris. The river did not look as daunting as it had the day before. Its banks were lined with rushes and reeds of all kinds. The child let go of her hand and ran down to the river's edge. The water birds rose in unison, flapping and shrieking as they flew into the sky. The boy stopped by the water's edge, pointing to fresh new shoots of edible reed. They were soon feasting on the crisp white ends of the shoots, quite oblivious to the clouds of insects enveloping them or the snakes that lay coiled and ready just beyond their naked feet. Soon, as they waded through the thick grasses they discovered nests containing eggs. This place was a haven of culinary delights.

The mother was looking for a safe place to cross, but after walking with Noname for some time downstream she was confused. At one wide point of the river she had tried to ford across but the water proved too deep, with the water murky and hiding many dangers. They retraced their steps. When they reached their original place by the bank they stopped to rest. She put Noname on her breast while munching on some tender shoots. They moved on upstream. After some time, they came to a likely crossing place at the confluence of two small streams entering the river, near a bend. This section of the river had the advantage of a low sandy island halfway across where they could rest if necessary. On the opposite bank, she could see impressions where large animals had trampled down tall savanna grasses and even small eucalyptus, making huge swaths through the undergrowth. This is where they would cross. By the time they had crossed the river, it was late afternoon. The pair continued until sunset, tired and weary.

The afternoon had been sweltering and humid. Clouds of insects, attracted by large dung patties swarmed around them. She used the ochre in her pouch to smother their faces as protection from the ravenous onslaught and a paddle-shaped branch to dig into the soft earth to form a shallow depression. She covered the created space with dry grasses and undergrowth as best she could. They spent two uncomfortable nights in the depression, listening to the strange bellowing of unknown beasts, and retching on the stench of rotting manure.

One morning, Noname was on her breast but he was not satisfied. They were both undernourished. He was crying, and uncooperative. She was thirsty. She would have to find fresh water. She knew the little stream that joined the big river was to her left. Although it was not quite in the direction she wanted to travel she became desperate to locate it. The further from the river they went the terrain became less difficult, with widely spaced large eucalyptus with an underlay of low shrubs and tussock grass. By mid-morning, they were both dehydrated and Noname had cried himself to sleep still clinging to his mother's back.

Eventually, she came to the little creek with clear water still flowing. With a cry of relief, she put her son down. They both drank until they could drink no more. They feasted on honey ants, termites, and the nectar of colourful flowers. They remained there for two days recovering from the ordeal of their journey from the river. She had surveyed the land and could see that the stream led towards the grey-blue hills that could be seen in the distance. She sang a song for the stream and danced for her old medicine man, Yaramaa, as Noname looked on enchanted. The great blue hills on the horizon beckoned her with both menace and with love.

On the fourth morning after their crossing, they were refreshed and ready to move on. They started along the muddy creek bed. Noname walking beside his mother. They were in no hurry and welcomed a chance to meander through nature's realm, under the shade of eucalyptus with dense thickets of tall cabbage palms interspersed with a variety of mulga and messmate. There was an undergrowth of fine tussock grass where they could sleep comfortably. They walked on admiring the brilliant rainbows shimmering through the canopy. Light rain showers washed their bodies of dust as they journeyed. Scores of butterflies flickered overhead landing softly on them, as tiny marsupial mice scampered around their feet.

Noname gorged on mulga apples. His mother nibbled on seeds and sweet roots. Late one day, they became aware of a cacophony of sound in the surrounding trees. Within a few minutes, they were confronted by a flock of enormous flightless birds standing three times the height of an adult human. The dozen or so birds were unlike any birds they had ever seen or dreamt of. They had large heads, black beady eyes, and thick rounded beaks of brilliant yellow. Their necks were long, their bodies rounded and supported by long sturdy legs. Some appeared to have their heads buried in the dirt. Among the alien birds were their chicks who looked at them without any apparent fear. One chick was tangled in a briar and was struggling to free itself. Its feathers lost in the dust.

The mother approached it carefully and with considerable effort freed it from the briar. Noname looked on concerned, still overwhelmed by the size of these harmless giants. The chick ran off and they proceeded on their way; Noname talking and gesturing to his mother about their extraordinary experience. With a clutch of feathers secured under her belt, the mother sang a song to the ancestors and spirits.

That day they made camp early, near the stream and in the shade of Cabbage Fan Palms, while she had her period. Noname had found ground nuts and a variety of fruit for his mother to enjoy. After two days they moved on. The landscape was uniform and flat, with open forest giving way to grassy woodlands and low scrub. The blue-grey hills shimmered in the heat of the day. Shielding her eyes she looked carefully. She discovered that the blue-grey hills were actually several huge rocks, rounded by erosion which from a distance had merged into one. She could see at the base a thin green line of rainforest in front of crumbling cliffs.

Suddenly, they were ankle-deep in plagues of marsupial mice rushing headlong, in one great mass of squeaking, mayhem, towards the rocks. Noname screamed, trying to rid himself of the mice climbing over his body. They moved on at a faster pace avoiding the mice as best they could. She was hot and flustered when she tripped and fell face down into a long shallow depression. She screamed. Noname came running. In front of his mother was an enormous snake, covered in brightly coloured scales. Its huge, fat, bloated body flowing out of the depression and onto the ground above. It had a small head quite out of proportion to the size of its body. For a moment its bright sharp eyes looked at her; its mouth open as it caught and munched on an avalanche of mice. Blood oozed from the corners of its mouth. She looked at this creature with revulsion. She clambered out of the

depression, grabbed Noname by the hand, and screaming ran as fast as she could from the ghastly apparition.

It took them three days to reach the rocks. The distance had been deceptive. They came at first to a low rocky escarpment, devoid of interest. They walked on into the delights of the rainforest at the base of the sandstone cliffs. Many varieties of trees occupied this space close to the protection of the rocks. Great vines entwined themselves between the highest trees. Ferns, mosses, and fungi occupied the forest floor. Filtered light and rotting wood encouraged the growth of orchids of all kinds. Strange and colourful birds flitted through the canopy, while big aggressive flightless birds with black and blue feathers, and long legs, browsed through the forest floor. But the mother was cautious, her confrontation with the rainbow snake had shaken her confidence. They were in unknown territory. There were sounds and smells of alien beasts. There were strange fungi in this forest, things she would never eat. She had to find a safe place to look out and rest. She must safeguard her son.

Climbing up the crumbling face of a cliff, the mother discovered a wide smooth ledge under an overhang. It was high enough to see over the tops of the canopy and onto the plain beyond. She made them comfortable by placing dry straw and leaves on the base of the ledge. By weaving thin vines together she made a long rope. She then secured the rope to a rock on the ledge and trailed it down the broken rock face. It made an excellent guide to their newly created home. She had time to contemplate their situation.

She was missing the company of her band- the marsh tribe, and the medicine man, who had taught her the law of the ancestors. A law that proclaimed that women did not hunt or make fire and that women always made themselves available for the needs of men. Furthermore, no new ways were to be introduced without tribal permission. She knew the men of her tribe, who stubbornly clung to the remnants of their home in the marshes, now becoming inundated by the sea. Would they ever come? Would she ever see other human beings again? In the mornings after gathering food from the forest floor, she would sit and watch from her lookout over the vast plain before her. She could see herds of animals in the distance, but no sign of humans. Every night she heard terrible howls of ravenous creatures and the dying screams of massive animals. These sounds terrified her. Noname would sometimes wake up from a nightmare, sweat pouring from him. She would hold him tight, stroke and comfort him. They were one, mother and son.

One day, while Noname was playing elsewhere on the rocks, she looked down and saw a beast she did not recognise. It was not overly large, but lithe and muscular with long powerful legs. It was orange in colour with brown stripes lying sideways across its back. It had a large head with wide green eyes, a massive mouth showing sabre teeth, and a powerful jaw. A terrifying image to behold. It looked up from the trees and fixed its eyes on her. She had no defence against such a creature except resolve. The creature moved quickly, startling her and bound up the rocks towards her. She must face this predator bravely. She armed herself with large round stones, one in each hand. She prepared to fight.

The lion raced towards her; running up the broken rocks at speed, roaring and gnashing its teeth. She stood her ground on the edge of the platform. She was sure her end had come. Leaping up towards her with its mouth open, the marsupial lion sprung. She let loose her stones. From above a spear tore into the lion's flesh. It lay dead. She looked up amazed to see a small swarthy man standing on top of the overhang.

"My name is Tan, said the man smiling, I've been looking for you since the river."

She knelt in submission and relief, realising that she did not understand a word he said.

A fire was always burning in a hearth of stones in the middle of the ledge. It was daunting to both spirits and snakes at night. The fire cooled down to embers as the night closed in. Tan reached over to turn two large goannas that were roasting in the coals of the fire. Noname could see faces reflected in the firelight. The new people. Tan's family had invited themselves to share their home on the ledge. Tan had two wives and two daughters. The daughters were both on the verge of becoming women. Two young men had secured them as possessions. Noname thought of these men as Stoneface, and the other man as Longlimp given he was tall and walked with a limp since birth. Noname kept close to his mother while he closely watched the interaction between the new group. The men took turns sleeping with the young girls, Wallah and Tush. Sometimes swapping places during the night. Tan only slept with one of his wives, the one he called Nan. The other wife named Fi, slept by herself away from the group. Nan was short and swarthy like Tan. She had long dark brown hair which she kept in place with sharp triangular pieces of bird bone.

She tied it at the back of her neck and secured it with a thin vine. She became friends with Noname and his mother. Nan helped her with her hair, cutting and thinning it out using sharp fragments of animal bone. Nan would call his mother Sepi. Noname felt possessive towards his mother. The intrusion of this new family had made Noname jealous. He watched his mother look longingly at Tan while Nan taught her their language. He was interested in Tan's spears with hardened tips. He had never seen spears so long before. He went to sleep with his mother always holding a small sharp piece of stone. He wished they would go away until he remembered the lions, who kept up a screaming howl during the night from their dens among the rocks.

During the day, Noname would sit or lie with Tan's second wife Fi, who would occupy herself singing and beating sticks together in a monotonous rhythm. Sometimes she would shake, and sweat profusely. Noname would gather water from pools in the rocks. He would drip it over her face and let her drink from his hands. She would smile at him. When Fi felt better she would teach him words of their language.

"She is sick," he would plead with his mother.

"I'm not a medicine woman," his mother would say.

But the cold was in Fi's body and she would shudder, sweat and go into delirium. One morning, Tan got the blood of snakes and mixed it with brown dust, clay, and water. The band covered themselves in this paint and sang and danced on the ledge, all day and all night. Noname sat and watched by the firelight in the far corner of the ledge.

Noname would sometimes amuse himself by playing with stones large and small. The majority were the brown-coloured stones crumbly and soft, but others were different, having blue-grey streaks. These were very hard and Noname found that the ones with sharp edges could be used for sharpening the tips of spears. Tan was pleased and showed Noname that by burnishing the spear tips in the fire, and by constantly turning the tips they would brown nice and hard; hard enough maybe to pierce the thick hides of the large stumpy animals that grazed in herds far off on the plains, in the direction of the setting sun. This was the direction his mother would look toward while sitting cross-legged on the ledge. Looking for their band. Looking for their people. If only they would come.

The second wife was dying. It was a dark night, and Fi was sitting leaning back against the young boy. Coverings discarded. Only the firelight illuminated the scene. Nan and Sepi were by her side as she lay in Noname's arms. The young girls were crying and sitting at second wife's feet. The men stood in a circle around her.

"Do not open my head or bones," she said softly.

Shortly after her head rolled to one side. Noname gently laid her body down. There was a great silence, broken only by the girls weeping and the sound of nocturnal creatures scurrying about in the forest below.

"Dig," ordered Nan.

The men found flat stones, but the ground on the ledge was too hard for them and they soon gave up. Noname had a collection of sharp bone pieces. He fetched a sharp heavy bone and began to dig. He was now taller, growing muscular, and strong. He dug with a frenzy.

$$\diamond$$

The other men joined in with large sharp bones following his lead. By day's end, a deep hole had been dug in the softer earth at the back of the ledge.

Tan took a rock and smashed the body's skull. Each took it in turn to eat some brain. Noname and Sepi refused. Tan cracked the two thigh bones. The group used thin sticks to extract the marrow, all ate, except for Noname and his mother. Although the body of Fi was mutilated it was carried with reverence and placed beside the newly dug grave. Stoneface and Longlimp collected kindling from the forest floor and brought it to the ledge. Two large pieces of rotting tree trunk were hauled up to the ledge and ignited. Immediately, black and toxic smoke bellowed and swirled throughout the cave-like interior of the ledge. The rising sun threw the scene into shadows of despondency. It was midday before the smoke cleared and sunlight penetrated the home of the little band. They placed the body of Fi in the grave as Nan poured water over the deceased's face.

"Drink when you are dry," she said.

They all filed by, repeating the action. Nan placed fruit and nuts in the grave.

"Eat, wife, when you are hungry," she said.

This action was repeated by the others. Nan whispered something to Sepi. She spoke to her son. With the help of the others, Noname started to sweep the earth into the hole covering the body.

"Wife has returned to the ancestors," said Nan.

Many seasons passed. Now the wet season lasted longer, the dry shorter. During the day, the heat and humidity was unbearable. Huddled on the ledge the band wondered if it would ever stop raining. The dank rainforest was growing at a prodigious rate. The forest floor always such a great source of food was no longer serving their meagre needs. The forest floor became dark as sunlight failed to penetrate the dense vegetation. Nothing would grow there. The band was starving.

Noname had grown into a tall strong boy, now taller than Tan. He was proud and carried a full-sized spear and a sharp stone in a pouch attached to his woven belt. Going out at night with long spears, Tan, Noname, Stoneface and Longlimp would go out hunting; out of the forest and onto the plain, always wary of the danger from the aggressive purple birds, and lions. They sometimes caught anteaters feasting on the many termite mounds, but food was still scarce. Tan held a council. The plan was to go further out onto the plain to hunt the huge animals that Tan called whom-tak. These beasts grazed on the plain in herds. Tan had never hunted the whom-tak before, it had never been necessary. One moonlit night, the four warriors set out across the plain; they picked their way over difficult terrain, wet underfoot and studded with low vegetation. Noname was not convinced the plan would work, but he had no say, no say at all.

Over the following hours, they moved forward stealthily until close to daybreak, when they were confronted by a huge beast partially hidden in a hollow. The animal had stubby legs, a thick fat body covered in thin wispy brown hair and a large black snout. It saw them, lifting its head and displaying its cavernous mouth and sharp incisor teeth. It roared.

Noname remembered what his mother had told him 'Never run in the face of danger.' He stood his ground as the beast rushed past him knocking him to the ground, and scrambled up just in time to throw his spear at its hindquarters. His aim was true but the barb had no effect, the spear bouncing off the thick brown hide. He was hurt and shaken. Wiping off the dirt, he could see blood flowing from a gash on his arm and a deep graze down his side. The animal crashed through the undergrowth in pursuit of the others. Then a distant scream. He could do nothing to help. To his left, partly hidden in the undergrowth, Noname spotted the animal's burrow. A young whom-tak was nestled in the straw and whimpered at the intrusion. It had thick white skin. Noname retrieved his spear only to find that the tip was broken. He quickly sharpened the spear with his flint, then thrust his spear into the young animal's side. He checked that it was dead. He threw the young whom-tak over his shoulder. Now for the long and painful walk to the ledge, in the heat and humidity of the coming day.

Noname arrived back, in the late afternoon, hot and exhausted. He was greeted warmly. His mother bathed his wounds. Tan and Stoneface placed the dead whom-tak in the coals of the fire. While Noname was resting in the protection of the overhang, he could detect an air of despondency. He could hear Nan playing the sticks and singing in a monotonous rhythm. He knew what it meant. It was too painful to move so he called out to Tush. Both girls came to him and they cradled him in their arms crying and softly wailing. Tush spoke.

"Tan say Longlimp dead crushed by whom-tak." She was crying.

Noname could see that she was pregnant.

"He favourite man," said Tush, as an afterthought.

Wallah came close to Tush and held her tightly. Wallah spoke, pointing accusingly at Noname.

"You stupid men going hunting so far from ledge."

He rolled over on the soft bed they had made for him. Looking out over the ledge he could see his mother sitting cross-legged and looking out over the moonlit plain. Towards the west. Nan added more kindling to the fire.

Tan and Stoneface started to butcher the roasted whom-tak with sharp stones. They sat round the fire eating in silence. They had been starving and now their bellies were full. Nan started to wrap the little remaining meat and offal in thick leaves. She silently stored the food. They all watched her fit the parcels of whom-tak, into cracks in the rocks. The naked women covered themselves in red ochre and for many hours they sang and danced to the spirits of the ancestors. When the ceremony was over his mother came to him, he stood up and clung to her. She kissed him on the lips, she noticed his erection.

"You are a man, you must have the initiation rites of men', she whispered.

"Tonight I sleep with Tan," she added.

Noname stood, fury in his eyes. How dare he take my mother; how dare he run from danger, and how dare he ignore Longlimp's passing. Tomorrow there must be a reckoning.

That night, Noname dreamt a powerful dream. He saw the spirit of Longlimp in the form of a shooting star flying through the heavens towards the Milky Way, shining with fire. He saw many spears tipped with blood. From high above the earth he saw mountains, rivers, and the Rainbow Serpent enmeshed in the totality of the land and its creatures. Then he was falling, falling. He awoke. His dream world stayed with him long into the night.

But he was still in shock, and the pain of the deep graze to his side still racked him. Someone came over and gave him meat.

Soon Noname's thoughts turned to the initiation ritual that could not be delayed any longer. He could see that in the stars. He knew he had no power, the law was the law, and he would need to go through the initiation ritual of manhood. Tan came to him.

"It will be in three days prepare yourself," he said.

Noname thought of asking his mother, then his anger returned, the thought of her sleeping with Tan was abhorrent to him. He rose and slowly walked over to Nan and sat beside her.

"What do I have to do?" he asked.

"Keep away from the woman and recover from your wound. Now lie on your side," she directed.

Nan then applied a soothing lotion and some mint leaves to the wound. Nan continued.

"Now you must isolate yourself. Find another place on the rock to sleep and remember to stay away from all the females on the ledge."

The rain had stopped. Noname had found a small ledge of sandstone about halfway down the rock they called their home. He scooped out a shallow hole under the ledge just wide enough for him to sleep, then went down through the dense undergrowth to the rainforest floor in search of food. He found some tasty fungi and two tree frogs which he gutted and flattened and placed in the sun to dry. He enjoyed the fresh fungi, then lay on the ledge to rest and wait for nightfall.

Looking up at the stars Noname went into a shallow sleep. He dreamt. It was a vivid jumble of images and distorted memories. He was being thrust violently up and down in space as he tried to avoid logs that fell across his path, along with spears that showered towards him. He was falling and reached out to save himself, waking with a start. He lay motionless until dawn avoiding the risks that sleep might bring.

The next day was the day of the initiation. Stoneface came to him and said.

"There is much joy in the camp. Tush has given birth to a boy, new people have arrived, "You will be expected tomorrow at midday for the initiation."

And so Stoneface went back to the camp, his mission completed.

The next morning, Noname searched for food again in the dank rainforest but only found orchids which he stripped, eating the bulbs. He climbed up to his temporary home and waited for midday. Then he reluctantly made his way over the rocks and crannies he knew so well for the initiation to manhood, which he knew would mean pain and humiliation.

At the furthest end of the ledge, by the rockfall, Noname saw five naked men covered in black ochre and wearing masks. The woman must be hidden but close at hand, he thought. He could hear a baby crying. The men approached him beckoning him to kneel. The short man in the middle was easily recognisable, despite the mask, it was Tan.

One man held his head steady. With a powerful blow, Tan knocked out Noname's top front tooth using a sharp piece of hardwood and a rock. Blood issued from his mouth. Four great cuts were scourged into his back. He remained silent. Then he was pushed towards the fire and there held until the hairs on his arms and legs were singed off. Tan then called out,

"We name you, Jaborri."

It was over, the five men walked off singing and chanting and took the way of the rockfall to the rainforest below. Noname stood defiant. Shortly afterwards, the woman appeared from their hiding place and moved towards him, but he held up his hand; he was not ready for whatever came next. He went back to his place on the rocks.

After a day, Nan came to him dressed his wounds, and brought him the last of the meat. It was fly-blown and covered in maggots, regardless, he ate it all. Nan spoke.

"You were hungry."

"Who are the new people?" he asked.

"They are from our band, hunters and their woman, they came looking for us,"

"What does Jaborri mean?"

"Man of the spirits," said Nan.

"I like it well enough," Noname replied.

"Come back to the ledge, the women are waiting for you, all those who are able will give themselves to you,"

"No, I need time in solitude." Nan was impatient.

"You don't have time, we are starving. You owe that to me, and to Tan."

"I hate Tan."

"Why?"

"Because he has my mother." Nan threw up her hands in frustration.

"She is only second wife since Fi went to the ancestors, I'm first wife and medicine woman."

But Jaborri was insistent.

"Be that as it may, but I still want to move south into the plains where the whom-tak roam. I will travel south with anyone who will follow me."

She looked at him with disbelief, for it was true they could no longer stay on the ledge, but could Jaborri lead a band? He continued,

"I will stay here for two more days and live off the fungi in the forest, then come back and choose those who will follow me, you will be my first, it has to be."

Nan looked at him in astonishment.

"This will mean someone will die," she warned.

It had been a glorious morning, with a spectacular sunrise. Voluminous clouds drifted across the sky, indicating the end of the wet and the advent of cooler weather. Jaborri clambered onto the ledge to be immediately confronted by Tan and the new men. He thought they looked haggard, skinny, and drawn. Jaborri knew it was now or never, and with a sharp stone clenched in his fist he smashed a right hook into the face of Tan. Tan fell to the ground unconscious. The other men ran off towards the rockfall and disappeared.

Only Stoneface stood fast, grinning. They both began to laugh. The two new women, who had been standing together with the others came forward and embraced him. One by one, they gave him their bodies; very slowly, so he would not spill his seed. The last woman to approach was Nan. She rode him with abandon, until at last their lust was satisfied.

The women's attention turned to Tan who still lay prostrate. Sepi took him, cradling him in her arms. Wallah brought him water and sat him up. But blood was still gushing from his mouth, he could not drink. He looked at them with terror in his eyes. He started to choke, turned blue and began to thrash about. And then his body lay still. Nan walked over and knelt by his side. She wiped the blood from his chest and placed an ear to his heart. Nan spoke.

"He has gone to the ancestors, we shall bury him next to Fi."

"Not so!" said the commanding voice of Jaborri.

"He shall be buried on top of the overhang facing towards his tribe, towards the east."

"So be it," said Nan in a whisper.

Jaborri looked at his mother still cradling the body of Tan in her arms. Sepi returned his gaze.

"I shall never leave the ledge, give me back this tracker, the man who saved my life," she screamed.

"The spirits of the dreaming and their law shall determine all things. I shall follow the whom-tak. All those who stay will either starve or be eaten alive by lions. Those who want to follow me, prepare yourselves for a long journey."

Then there was silence, broken only by the rushing wind from the beating wings of a great black bird that circled high above.

The next day, Stoneface and Jaborri set to work preparing a burial space for Tan's body. They climbed to the top of the overhang and found a shallow dip in the rock. This they enlarged by scraping the softer sandstone with hard flint. It was not deep enough by day's end so they went back to the ledge to rest. Some of the women had been foraging and had come back to camp with tree nuts and cabbage palm kernels. They ate and were soon asleep after an exhausting day.

Stoneface and Jaborri started again at sunrise, scraping and scraping into the sandstone until they were sure the grave was deep enough. Tomorrow, Tan would be buried. All the band would be on top of the overhang to witness the sunrise break forth magic rays of hope. Two large flat stones would be hauled over the grave, and the women would paint themselves with white pigment and dance the dance of the ancestors, to the rhythm of the sticks.

✦

The new day dawned. Nan had made water containers from the whom-tak innards. Tush had woven a basket to honour the baby, and Wallah had made awes and pins. At a distance, Sepi made amulets. The two new women had collected ochre, wrapping it in cabbage tree leaves. Jaborri and Stoneface made spears, clubs, and fire sticks. Early in the morning, they scrambled their way down the rockfall for the last time into the dark, morbid, forest, all feeling a sense of foreboding. Only Sepi had stayed behind on the ledge.

There had been an emotional parting between mother and son, with Sepi giving Jaborri his totem, an amulet containing part of an eagle's claw. Jaborri broke his mother's embrace and walked away disguising his tears.

The small band continued the journey. There were five women, a baby, and two men. Jaborri in front leading the way, Stoneface at the back protecting the rear. They made their way along a well-known track until the thinning trees allowed some light to illuminate the way. Slowly, the great plain opened before them, sunlight bathing the grassland with glorious hues of greenery, consisting of shrubs and flowers in a blaze of colour. They walked out for some time until Stoneface came running up shouting to Jaborri,

"It's Sepi, she's coming!"

They all stopped and looked around. At a distance, Sepi could be seen running and waving her arms. Jaborri was alarmed.

"Get into a defensive posture," he warned, handing out spears.

"There may be lions."

Sepi arrived laughing and out of breath.

"The whom-tak have gone. Every one of them,"

They all looked at her in amazement.

"I thought I'd better come with you," she said. "I'm no friend of lions."

They followed the tracks of the whom-tak and the terrain was easy-going given most of the trees and shrubs had been flattened or uprooted by the herd. On the second day of their march, they came to the end of the line of rocky hills that gradually petered out into a low flat escarpment. Here the great herd of whom-tak had wheeled around to the left, skirting the end of the rocks and heading east. The going was hard without the wide tracks cut by the whom-tak. The terrain was rocky in part or covered by low yet dense scrub. They only had one small stone hatchet and three flint knives to cut their way through. Water was not a problem as many small creeks and streams flowed from the rocks. The women dug up tough old tuberous roots, and small flowers to eat. The men burned off leeches as they forded numerous water courses.

Jaborri was increasingly concerned about his mother. Over recent months, she had aged perceptibly and dawdled at the back of the group. Jaborri began to regret that he had killed Tan. He had been a good bushman and tracker and his mother had doted on him. She missed him and rarely spoke to the others. Jaborri now realised he had acted impulsively. He looked towards the night sky and sought understanding from the morning star.

$$\Diamond$$

I t was then that he decided there should be a morning ritual dance. Women and men would dress in grass skirts, and paint themselves with ochre. They would dance to the spirit of the great Rainbow Serpent which had created the landscape and all its creatures. Then all would be as it should be.

One night, Jaborri was woken by the smell of burning. He went up to the lookout and saw a fire burning in the west. It soon became a massive conflagration. A strong southerly wind carrying all before it. They stood and watched the flames roaring into the night sky. Stoneface spoke to Jaborri.

"I think others started it."

"Yes, that must be," said Jaborri.

"We will investigate in the morning." And so they did.

The little band left early the next day and followed a dry water course west. Jaborri and Stoneface stopped, they needed to talk. They were close enough to see the devastation caused by the fire.

"Should we go on?" asked Stoneface.

"The fire has gone, now only smoke and ash," said Jaborri.

"No not that," replied Stoneface,

"Are we ready to confront others and how do we know they will be a friendly tribe?" Jaborri thought about this and called his mother over. He embraced her and looked into her eyes.

"We have been through so many trials together… You have always looked to the west for your people, how can we be sure it is them?"

She put her fingers to his mouth. She took a deep breath and cupping her hands to her mouth sang, "Hoia-ho, hoia-ho, wigimajara," She sang, She waited. She tried again.

"Hoia-ho, hoia-ho, wigimajara," She called again. They all waited. Then there was a sharp and unmistakable call, repeating the song several times.

"They are my people. We have found them at last," she cried with great joy.

The head man of the marsh tribe, Derridaa, beckoned to New-man.

"Do you know that song?"

"No, not my language," New-man replied.

Derridaa called the band together.

"Who knows the voice, singing in our language?"

An old man shuffled forward, and holding his right hand high, spoke in a faltering voice.

"It is the voice of the woman who fled the waters."

He then coughed and spat on the earth. There was a collective gasp of astonishment.

"We shall call out to them and we of the marshes shall beat the rhythm, sing our songs, blow the drone pipes to welcome them," said Derridaa.

But the old man held up his hand, his fist clenched.

"I remember now, she has a son," He coughed. "He has a powerful totem…..,"

"If he lives he has the power of the second sight and the strength of eagles. Beware!"

Jaborri and Stoneface were watching from a distance. They then waved their group forward, picking their way through the blackened undergrowth to the campsite of the marsh band. Sari began singing at the top of her voice, the two new women giggling with glee. Both sides broke into a run, then embraced each other in a hubbub of joy and chatter. Sari found the old man and stood before him.

"Greetings Yaramaa," she said.

He embraced her, then stood back.

"Your son?" he asked, nodding toward Jaborri.

"Yes," she replied.

"Then I will not go on, it is here that I must go to the ancestors," he said, falling into her arms.

Jaborri approached them through the throng of dancing gyrating couples.

"This is my tribe's medicine man, Yaramaa, he is overcome with emotion," said Sari. Jaborri touched the old man's head running his hand across the thin and balding scalp.

"Help me lay him down, careful now he's very frail," she said.

And so they laid him on a patch of sand swept clear by the evening breeze. He half sat up and stretching out a hand touched the amulet around Jaborri's neck, before lying down in the dust.

"You have powerful magic," said a voice behind them.

They stood up and looked into the eyes of someone who looked vaguely familiar.

"They call me New-man, I was at your manhood initiation on the ledge."

"Yes I remember," said Jaborri.

"You and another ran off."

"Yes, after travelling for many days in the bush we found this band."

"And what of the other?" said Sari.

"He was speared for stealing a woman," was the tart reply.

Days passed. Jaborri had built a windbreak of branches and stringy bark with a roof of grass tufts and wiled away the time there with his mother Sari, Nan, Tush and the baby, usually painting on paperbark trying new and interesting pigments. There was food aplenty. The women used digging sticks to prod the burnt-out bush to find juicy goannas, snakes, green spring roots and turtles.

But Jaborri was becoming frustrated. He had not been invited to attend the council of the elders, which had been going on for many days. There were ongoing arguments among those attending about which direction to follow. When the elders announced they would be travelling west, Jaborri had had enough, he was boiling with anger. He confronted Yaramaa, who had miraculously recovered.

"I'm travelling south with anyone who wishes to follow. I'm on the earth of the Rainbow Serpent, my course is governed by my totem," he called out.

Behind Yaramaa were spear-carrying hunters watching on from a distance.

"All remember my warning," screamed Yaramaa, his voice raising to a crescendo.

"This boy without a beard defies the elders."

Jaborri dodged the first spear to go flashing past. Then Stoneface was beside him. He thought their end had come. Another spear flashed between them which they easily avoided. Then Derridaa was there, raising both arms aloft. The spearmen dropped their spears. Jaborri turned to look at Stoneface. "Hold fast," he whispered.

The evening was closing in when Derridaa addressed the confrontation.

"Go back to your campsites," he ordered.

So the people started to drift away, returning to their family groups. Jaborri and Stoneface had held their ground.

"My group will perform our morning dance in two days" announced Jaborri.

"May the spirits be with you," said Derridaa.

In the light of the campfire, Jaborri explained to those assembled, Sari, Wallah and Stoneface, Nan, New-man, women one and two, Tush and her baby, and several others who would also join them, how to perform the morning dance, and how to make the grass skirts that all would wear. There was much to prepare and so much depended on it. His mother had been sick during the day, but only that night did he realise that she was pregnant. Maybe it's the essence of Tan that's within her, he thought.

Two days later at the rising of the morning star, they sang and danced with passion and agility. One row of men, and one of women all painted with the finest white ochre, danced to the rhythm of the clap-sticks. All those watching were enthralled. The woman threw dust into the air; singing and shouting, with the deep drone pipe adding to the monotonous and exciting rhythm, their bodies wildly swirling to a climatic conclusion. Finally, they all lay on the ground exhausted. There was spontaneous applause from children and adults alike.

Standing up, Jaborri, always vigilant, could see Yaramaa turning away. He ran after him through the crowd, Nan following.

"Old man," he shouted.

"Are your eyes so bad that you cannot see the great scars on my back, my missing tooth, my scorched and blistered body that I endured in silence to become a man?"

There was no reply. Nan reached out and held him, kissed him, and put her hand to his mouth.

"What is done is done," she spoke quietly, with tears in her eyes.

When she looked up she froze. Jaborri looked around, they were surrounded by spearmen, who promptly discarded their spears and with a great shout lifted him up on their shoulders, to the delight of the assembled crowd.

The dance solidified their position, it made them an entity separate from the marsh band. It gave them decision-making powers. They decided to follow the burnt bush south, against the wishes of the men of the marshes. The fire had made walking easy, with plenty of opportunity for finding animals like hopping creatures that the marsh band called terrimunka, and other foodstuffs amongst the vast expanse of blackened tree trunks and ash. They walked for days to the end of the fire-ravaged bush. Then, when the wind was right, they lit another fire to smooth their path. They walked for many days using the same endless pattern.

One day, Stoneface who had been scouting ahead, suddenly appeared from behind a stand of unburnt trees waving his arms and shouting. Spearmen ran to help.

"There are giant terrimunka, twice the height of a man," Stoneface reported.

Jaborri and the others caught up.

"There is danger," yelled Stoneface. "Huge beasts!"

And then, to the astonishment of the band, a giant terrimunka approached from behind a stand of trees that had been untouched by the fire. It strode along towards them, its long, claw-tipped arms outstretched. It loped forward on massive legs. Its flat and ugly face menacing. They all looked on, paralysed with fear. Then for an instant, time stood still.

From the corner of his eye, Jaborri detected a flash, a momentary glint, high overhead. He looked again, there was a clear sky with a few streaky clouds. He heard a scream. At that instant, he was pushed aside. He caught his balance, and looking through the melee of running people saw the giant terrimunka lying prostrate on the ground, a spear protruding from its chest.

The band filed past to inspect the giant, some intent to smell and touch it. Jaborri regaining his composure held up his hand amongst the hubbub.

"This shall be a sit-down place. This shall be a story place."

When order had been restored, he spoke.

"Who threw the spear?"

A man stood up at the back.

"New-man, you threw the spear? Where did that come from?"

New-man responded,

"I have made a spear thrower, my people use them, it gives the spear a much greater range, force, and accuracy."

"But this is our law, that no new things should be allowed," said Jaborri.

While the debate continued some had butchered parts of the terri-munka, the short stumpy tail proving good eating when roasted on a fire. They remained at the sit-down place, only moving camp to escape their excrement, and for the women to find food.

The men accepted the spear thrower into their law. And over many years they proceeded to make and perfect the woomera. This is a story place they agreed, the first giant terrimunka killed, and the first use of the spear thrower by a member of the band. One evening, by their campfire, Jaborri was in the arms of Nan.

"Something worrying me," he said, kissing her neck.

"Oh, don't worry about me, my baby will come when it's ready."

She looked radiant and serene.

"I was thinking whether I was a fit person to lead our band. When the time came for me to lead I froze, that time the huge terrimunka first appeared."

"No one is perfect, we all have our failings," Nan protested.

"And you have your best men to advise you, Stoneface, New-man, and Talltree."

"I feel it will soon be time to move on, to complete our journey," he added.

"Where are we going?" she said.

✧

"To a place like no other, to a place of peace and contentment, to a place of abundant fish and yams, to a place of love and comradeship, I have seen it in my dreams."

She looked at him in amazement, unable to reply.

They stayed in that place until Sepi had her baby, giving birth at the birthing tree. Jaborri checked his mother through a throng of women. He smiled at her and took the baby off the breast, the baby howling. It was small, swarthy, and wrinkled, with much hair throughout its tiny body.

"My brother has the spirit of Tan," he said.

Returning the child to the arms of his mother, his face flushed with anger.

The band moved on, travelling south, always south, behind a fire. The early section to negotiate comprised a gentle incline with a receding tree line and some rocky outcrops. After several days, they came to a precipice overlooking a wide green valley. They could hear the gentle rush of water. There was no obvious way down, so they camped near a small stream that bubbled and swirled over the cliff in a delightful waterfall, its spray, reflecting a multitude of colours. The men came back from hunting with a good variety of game, goannas, small terrimunka, birds, and eggs. This was a beautiful place to find, with breathtaking views and sunsets to behold, and small caves to shelter in during the heat of the day.

"Is this the place of your dreams?" asked Nan.

Jaborri took her in his arms and kissed her. He looked into her eyes.

"Eventually we will have to find a way down," he said with a smile.

The band spent many full and happy seasons near that place, spreading out in family groups along the top of the ridge. Jaborri found interesting flint and shaped it into useful tools. The woman looking after their children, Nan having given birth to another girl. The women also foraged for berries, plums, and nuts in the rocky ground above the valley. But the problem was firewood. Every day, the women had to travel further afield to find wood to burn for their cooking fires and hearths. And the nights were getting colder.

Eventually, the hunters found a place to descend into the green and lush valley below. The valley was damp and full of thinly spaced fern trees and tropical vegetation. It was inhabited by tiny songbirds, reptiles, small amphibians and mammals in abundance.

Shortly the hunters reported the tracks of several massive lizards of frightening proportions. Talltree spoke to the band.

"These lizards, if that's what they are, are the size of monstrous crocodiles."

New-man looking down, spoke in his quiet voice.

"It will be treacherous to cross the valley inhabited by these creatures, they will be carnivores of the most ferocious kind."

"They will be so well camouflaged, that's another problem," added Stoneface.

$$\diamondsuit$$

And yet this was the place where they had to cross if they were to proceed with their journey south. The valley stretched from east to west as far as the eye could see. And so, reluctantly, the decision was made, that despite the risks, they would move on.

The men, the elders of the tribe, would lead the band, moving into the valley when the wind was right. They would set fire to whatever would burn, slashing a path with the new axes Jaborri had made, killing snakes, and whatever else would stand in their path. Camping at night in the valley was fraught with danger, so they made temporary shelters and lit fires from whatever dry kindling they could find. Jaborri was determined and enthusiastic, he would let nothing stand in their way to cross the valley at all costs. On the second day, the band had made significant progress across the valley floor, hacking and burning a swathe through the undergrowth, when, unexpectedly, in a clearing not far from their encroachment and basking in the sun they spotted a giant carnivore lizard, It looked at them lazily. New-man steadied his spear and woomera, unsure where to aim, when Jaborri held up his hand. Some moments passed, then the huge lizard, yawning, turned away, crashing through the undergrowth and disappeared. They all burst out laughing.

"How did you know it wasn't dangerous?" they all jabbered.

"Well, it certainly was dangerous, but did you not see the size of its belly?" asked Jaborri, laughing.

"That thing had just had a good-sized meal."

They proceeded on, singing and giving thanks to the spirits of the ancestors who were guiding their path.

✧

Many full seasons had passed in succession. The passage of time slipping away without acknowledgement. Nan and Sepi were in a dry season shelter, their children in the dirt, playing together. They were camped on a featureless plain. All the men had gone hunting, except one man, Pariffinarra, who had joined the band with his wife Aap from the tribe of the marshes.

Sepi's child, Bornus was playing rough with the girl, she protested to her mother.

"Bornus pulls my hair and hurts me, I not like to play anymore!"

But Nan just laughed.

"He is a boy Alyaa, and can do whatever he likes with you, that is the law."

"Let's give them something else to do," suggested Sepi.

"They could help make goose eggs for a ceremony."

They went down to the waterhole ensuring the children would not contaminate the precious water. The children were shown how to make the eggs the correct size from the stiff sticky mud surrounding the water, leaving the eggs out to dry in the sun.

"Now when they are dry, you can paint them the correct colour for goose eggs," Sepi instructed the children.

"What colour is that?" asked Alyaa.

"Don't you remember," said Nan smiling.

"They are white. You will both paint your eggs with white pigment tomorrow."

"Why do we need eggs of mud, what use is that?" said Bornus.

Graham Schafer

"You must remember from the past, it's to ensure the continued existence of animals, and plants. These are the rituals we need to do, to increase the supply of natural species, you must learn this law from the men, it's important," said Nan.

By the time they got back to their shelter, the mud had mostly dried on the naked bodies of the children, both women scraping the mud off with wooden scrapers and wiping them clean with ducks down.

The children were ready for bed when Alyaa asked her mother,

"When can I have a baby mummer?"

"When you have become a woman."

"When will that be?" asked Alyaa.

"When you are much older," replied Nan.

"So how much older?" "Now let's see, you are now this many full seasons old," said Nan displaying six fingers.

"So maybe in another..." Nan holding up three fingers.

"How does the baby get inside you?" queried Alyaa, refusing to give up with her questions.

"A woman must lie under a spirit tree to receive a spirit child, then she must be mated with a man. We will make you a string tassel apron to show that you have not reached menarche."

"What is that?"

"When your spirit totem is defeated you will bleed, then you can join the other women in secret women's ceremonies."

This seemed to satisfy the young girl, who hugged her mother and fell fast asleep.

In the morning, after eating a variety of berries and fruit, it was time to paint the eggs of mud, Sepi mixing a beautiful thick white pigment.

"The men have been gone for a while," commented Nan.

"Yes it's strange, they had a men's secret gathering and then announced they would go hunting although we have plenty of food." Pariffinarra approached them. He was a thin elderly man with a white beard. He wore a red headband and large wooden ear-cylinders in the lobes of his ears.

"We will do a rainmaking dance when the men return," he announced.

"Yes," they said simultaneously.

"I shall arrange a husband for the girl," he announced.

Sepi and Nan greeted this information in silence.

"I have been made medicine man," he said.

"Where have the men gone?" said Sepi. As he walked off he called out.

"To the east, to the east."

The hunters had been tracking northeast for many days when they discovered signs of human activity, the ash of a fire and bones of a kill. The hunters were keen to disguise their body odour, so they smeared themselves with mud, and in a clearing, the newly initiated young hunters were shown how to apply burdock and nettle leaves under their armpits to soak up their sweat. They all wore emu feather thongs and carried spears, woomeras and baskets of honeycomb.

$$\diamondsuit$$

As quietly as possible, the hunters moved forward through this strange and eerie woodland, devoid of sound. Through a clearing, they watched women with their digging sticks, foraging in rolling undulating bushland.

Excitement grew amongst the new young hunters when suddenly they were ambushed. Three tribesmen jumped out of a hide brandishing short spears, clubs, and shields. They were short and swarthy, yelling and threatening the men in an unknown language. They indicated that they should go back until one man put down his spear and shield and approached Jaborri. He was sniffing with his nose in the air.

"He can smell the honey," said Jaborri speaking in their language.

"Greetings from afar," said Jaborri tentatively.

One man looked at him with suspicion.

"Fuck off," he said.

"Tan, Tan," said Jaborri.

This had an immediate effect. All the tribesmen now dropped their weapons and embraced Jaborri and others.

"We have come to trade honey for women," Jaborri continued. Negotiations continued. It was agreed that one basket of honeycomb for a young girl was fair, and two women per basket if the woman was old and past childbearing age.

But the young hunters became frustrated. For they could see that the foraging women had got wind of their danger. The young men could wait no longer. They broke away from the negotiation and ran toward the women. The women saw them and ran in all directions, screaming. They were no match for the lithe and fit hunters. Each woman was caught and bound, raped, cuffed about the face, and whipped about the buttocks.

"We will just take the young ones," called out Jaborri.

"Let the old ones go." Stoneface let out a cry.

"Tribesmen are coming! Get back to the trees!"

But the warning was too late. A spear flew through the air, its aim true. A young hunter was speared through the side of his body, killing him instantly. The tribesmen in the woods had been left to their own devices, so picking up a basket of honeycomb they ran for their lives, but to no avail. Jaborri, with a mighty throw of his spear and woomera, pierced the back of a fleeing man, who let out a scream, dying instantly. His precious honeycomb spilled out of the basket, to the delight of hordes of ants.

Jaborri and the hunters ran back to the trees and then took off the way they had come, hotly pursued by the tribesmen. Jaborri remembered his training, pulling up with Talltree, and Stoneface, they let fly a barrage of spears, until they were safe. After a day, they stopped to take stock. They had captured five young women, and an old one, but had lost all the baskets of honeycomb wrecked in the melee. Now to divide the women up. Talltree and Stoneface did not want a woman as they had wives. Jaborri chose two pretty young girls. Three young hunters got a woman each, the other hunters missed out, having to share the older women. They had lost one man, and another was wounded, speared in the leg.

After days of slow walking, carrying the wounded man, and feeding the captives, they reached their camp at last. Jaborri called out but the campsite was deserted. Despite their exhaustion, they set off at once to track the women and to find Pariffinarra.

After two days of tracking through tall tussock grasses, they found Pariffinarra. He was sitting in the shade of a small tree, chewing gum grubs, without a care in the world.

"We moved camp expecting your return," he said, looking up.

He gestured towards the captives.

"You have new women," said Pariffinarra, looking up and smiling.

The exhausted Jaborri simply nodded. He walked further on and found the women scratching rocks to make them bleed, and dancing a water ceremony. Sepi and Nan were on their knees digging a hole to find water. They stood up at his approach and looked at the hunters and captives.

"You've had a good hunt I see," said Nan. Jaborri approached her.

"That is my affair," he said, raising his voice.

He smashed her in the face and pushed her to the ground. He looked at Sepi.

"What's the use of a mother giving me an ugly brother, and what's the use of a wife who only gives girls? Both of you get out of my sight," he screamed.

Sepi helped Nan up. Sepi called out.

"The hole is dry, we have no water."

They walked off towards the women of the band.

Pariffinarra, Aap and Alyaa walked towards the tired hunters, who were resting parched with thirst.

"We shall do a rainmaking dance at once, prepare yourselves," said Pariffinarra.

"Rouse yourselves one last time brave hunters," called out Jaborri.

"Let the dance begin in accordance with our traditions."

Dark clouds could be seen on the horizon, rising above some misty mountains that offered no comfort or solace. The women held a secret woman's ceremony. Nan was a medicine woman and therefore had authority.

"The band has new women," said Nan, brandishing a black eye.

"We should welcome them to country with a ceremony."

"But these new women have been forced on us. They should be rejected," said another woman.

"And will you put a curse on the man who beat you?" asked another.

"As women, we have great power," said Nan.

"We can nurture or destroy life, and take revenge by magic, but these women have done no wrong. They will only strengthen the band by our acceptance."

Towards evening, the wind strengthened. Black and threatening skies riding ferocious gusts tore into the campsite. The squall bent trees and blew the topsoil into the sky, blackening their world.

All gasped in terror, except for Nan, who threw her arms in the air in thanks to the gods as the lightning and thunder rose to a climax. And then the rain came, blown in ferocious sheets of blinding maelstrom.

They drank their fill from muddy puddles, waterholes and fast-running creeks. The women of the band recovering their composure, sloshed through mud and debris, to find the six new women of the band. Nan welcomed them in their own language. Together the newly formed group found shelter, huddling together as best they could and waited for the dawn of a new beginning. The morning brought grey skies and humid conditions, with light showers of rain. Jaborri could see he had been outflanked by the women, and that he would need to make amends. Pariffinarra came to him carrying a broad leaf over his head and still trying to shake the moisture from his beard.

"We need to move, there may be reprisals."

"I know exactly what to do," replied Jaborri.

"And what is that?" queried Pariffinarra, looking at him with piercing eyes.

"We shall go south to the mountains," said Jaborri.

"For that is the place of the ancestral beings and totemic spirits, who will guide us to our destiny."

When they reached these mountains no ancestral beings could be seen or heard amongst those barren hills. So they moved on once more, realising that destiny is but a series of acts where all must press on regardless.

The children were older. Alyaa now nine years old had just been married to a newly initiated young hunter, Tarrurong. Bornus kept to his mother's hearth, Sepi teaching him the law of the marsh tribe. Their brief interaction with them, a fading memory. And then there was Walambar, the son of Stoneface. He was always close to Jaborri, who was teaching him the fine art of flint napping. The grown children seeming to thrive on travel and endless adventure.

Jaborri had settled down with his chosen young wives, Li, and Astya, who he loved passionately. They had both became pregnant simultaneously. When their time came both women gave birth to girls within a day of each other. Nan lived at Sepi's hearth with Bornus, but as a medicine woman, Nan assisted with both births. She kept the afterbirths as necklaces, they were powerful magic. Nan was content. Bornus would hunt for game with short spears, and the band would always have good food to share. One evening Nan and Sepi were sitting around the campfire alone.

"Two girls," said Sepi looking up and smiling at Nan.

"You have strong spirit powers from the ancestors."

"Yes," said Nan. "If they had been boys they would not have lived."

$$\diamond$$

The band travelled on over many seasons, and across hills and mountain ranges, stopping at some caves to paint images of their spirit ancestors. Bornus used a stopping place to plead with Sepi.

"I need my manhood ceremony, mamma, I need to be a man."

"You are not ready, your manhood is too soft, why are you in such a hurry to be a man?"

"Because I'm excluded from men's secret meetings, I want them to hear my voice."

Nan approached him.

"I think I can help, come with me," she said, putting her arms around him.

They walked out into the bush, but Nan could not find the right herbs. She took Bornus by the shoulders and facing him looked into his dark grey eyes.

"You are nearly as tall as me Bornus, you will soon be a man, what's this all about,"

"We are going the wrong way." He replied and stamped his feet on the ground in his frustration and anger.

"We should never have left the marsh tribe," he said. "They were our people."

Li and Astya were nursing their babies around the campfire. Jaborri was talking to Stoneface and Walambar about the day's hunt and how lucky they were to have caught a number of terrimunka, goannas, and an echidna. The woman bringing in good fat tubers and eggs.

"This is a good sit-down place," remarked Jaborri.

"We will remain here for a while I think."

Li and Astya nodded in agreement. That night, around another fire, Bornus, Sepi, Nan, Alyaa, and Tarrurong were eating roast terrimunka. It was a clear night, the stars were bright.

"I'm leaving." They all looked at Bornus.

"No don't go, you are like a big brother to me," said Alyaa.

"Where will you go," inquired Sepi?"

"I can tell you," said Nan. "He's going west."

"I will come too," called Tarrurong.

Both young men stood up and embraced, and after selecting spears, disappeared into the night.

Season after season the band crossed mountains and streams heading southeast. They lit fires to clear the land when necessary. Early one morning, as the sun was rising, Jaborri looking down from a hilly ridge noticed a bright reflection across the horizon of an otherwise featureless plain. He called Walambar and Stoneface.

"What do you make of it?" he asked.

Other members of the band soon joined them.

"It's a warning from the spirits," said some.

"We should not go on," said others.

As the day wore on, they were confounded by the spectacle before them, a series of huge lakes stretching across the plain, and with water birds in great numbers.

The boys raced on through the night, and unafraid, they stopped to rest at daybreak.

"What have you got?" said Bornus,

"Two spears, my amulet and some of Alyaa's hair," said Tarrurong laughing.

"I've got spears, a pouch with ochre, some flints in a leather belt and a water bag....."

"We have a long way to go so you had better find a way to carry water," said Bornus.

They clambered over rocky hills, one day merging into another. They learnt to make fire by striking the flints. The days became dry and increasingly hot. The rocky ground that burnt their feet now turned into red uncompromising sand.

"No one could live in this place, we should go back," said Tarrurong.

"But animals do live here, aren't we following the tracks of small rodents and sand goannas, even snakes," Bornus replied.

"I've hardly any water left in my skin." Tarrurong's resolve was starting to crumble. Further on, they found human footprints which were easy to follow. In the evening of the following day, when cautiously looking over the crest of a dune, they saw a tall dark man drinking from a waterhole near a deep cut in an outcrop of rock. His features were sharp, his eyes wide and large with straight black hair lying loose around his shoulders. He was thin and naked, except for a loin cloth. Neither of them had seen such a person before. He stood up and looking towards the crest of the dune beckoned to them.

"How did he know we were here? Asked Tarrurong.

"He is not of the marsh tribe, should we kill him?"

Graham Schafer

"Come, follow me," said Bornus.

They slid down the dune and stood some little distance from the man. Laying down their spears, Bornus spoke to him in the dialect of the east.

"We are happy to see a friend," Bornus offered.

The man said nothing, but walked over and inspected their spears, then ran his hand over each man's face and body. Nodding his approval, he beckoned them to follow.

"Why don't you try the language of the marshes?" asked Tarrurong.

"No, didn't you notice, there were ear cylinders tied around his neck," said Bornus.

They moved from waterhole to waterhole, picking up recruits, heavily armed with spears, shields and boomerangs. Further on they came to hilly saltbush country, and a dry salt lake. Their guide, who called himself Ooma, indicated that they should keep low and silent when approaching the brow of a ridge. Bornus and Tarrurong looked over. There was a large mob of people camped by the dry salt lake. They could see women, children, old and young. The women were getting water from a well.

"They are the marsh tribe," Tarrurong whispered to Bornus.

"Your mothers people."

Then the realisation struck Bornus, the marsh band before them was in mortal danger. But he could do nothing. Ooma was holding a knife to his throat. The desert tribe held back until nightfall. Then they fell on the unsuspecting people of the marshes. Using clubs, spears, and boomerangs they slaughtered them all. The boys looked down at the bloody carnage and wept, with the pitiful screams of the marsh people fresh in their ears they made off the way they had come, guided by Ooma, and carrying a message, never to trespass on the desert sands.

The band made their way to the shore of a lake and marvelled. The land was green and lush with many freshwater lakes interspersed with fine grassland and woods, where whom-tak grazed. Men, women, and children alike frolicked in the clear and warm waters. Water birds in great profusion and with a great flapping and squawking rose into the air.

All were happy washing away the dirt of so many seasons of travel. Fish swam in abundance. There were shellfish, yabbies, eggs of all kinds and sweet tender yams. The tribe made a camp on the banks of a lake, there was much excitement and chatter. All agreed that there should be a corroboree the very next day, and preparations began with elaborate body painting and the making of headdresses decorated with fine plumage.

J aborri was with his wives and children when Nan approached.

"Have you found your dream?" she questioned Jaborri.

"It's like a gift from the ancestors, my dream is satisfied, this is where I shall end my days," he replied.

Over the seasons, some men had been digging a channel between the lakes to trap fish. Other men had discovered a ridge of fine flint. Jaborri installed himself in the quarry to make fine stone points and blades, fine dust permeating his thick and lustrous beard. The women finding respite in the abundance of food and preparing secret ceremonies and dances.

In time, Bornus and Tarrurong found their way back to the band and marvelled at the bounty received from the ancestral spirits. There was a corroboree to tell the story of their safe return. A men's secret meeting was held, the women could not go near but could hear a great shout, and much singing of lament. No doubt the massacre of the marsh people was told and the existence of a new people who lived in the hot sandy desert was revealed.

Sepi spoke to Nan about the return of her son.

"He has changed," said Sepi. "He is sad, he will not talk to me. And Jaborri spends all his time in the quarry fashioning fine flints, and neglecting his wives."

"Yes, much has changed," replied Nan. "I will talk to them both."

Nan found Bornus, who was alone fishing in the lake. He came to her dropping his spear. They embraced, Bornus sobbing, tears cascading down his cheeks and onto Nan's shoulders and back. He shook, he cried, and then dropped to his knees. He looked up and gazed into Nan's eyes. She could not ask him and knew he could never tell the stories of men's secret business.

Nan walked to the quarry and found Jaborri, he was with Tarrurong. She sat down before them on the rocks.

"Tell me," she said. There was silence.

"Tarrurong! Tell me, TELL ME!"

He began to rock back and forth.

"They are all dead."

"Who?"

"The people of the marshes, the whole tribe were slaughtered by a new and fearsome tribe in the sandy desert."

Nan stood and embraced Tarrurong.

"I'm sworn not to tell," he said.

"Now I understand," said Nan. She turned to Jaborri.

"Jaborri what are you doing spending all your days at the quarry, we are both getting older and should spend our last days with our families."

"I'm going on another journey to take these fine flints to the tribes of the east in payment for the women we took............"

"A basket of fine flints in exchange for six women is a fair bargain don't you think?"

"Yes, indeed I do," said Nan with a smile.

"And please take your brother with you, he could help you on your travels."

Nan had tears in her eyes, how could she tell Sepi about the massacre of the marsh band?

And yet Nan carried love and hope in her heart. Nan walked out of the quarry and climbed to the top of a rocky outcrop. Nan looked towards the sun setting in a blaze of colour. Nan smiled again in wonder at the overwhelming beauty of the earth governed by the Rainbow Serpent and the spirit powers of the ancestors.

The End